Coffee: Hot
edited by Victoria Pond

Circlet Press, Inc.
Cambridge, MA

Coffee: Hot
edited by Victoria Pond

Printed in the United States.
ISBN: 978-1-61390-144-1

Print-on-demand edition.

For catalog, information about our imprints, review copies, and other information, please write to:

Published by:
Circlet Press, Inc.
39 Hurlbut Street
Cambridge, MA 02138

Or visit us online at: http://www.circlet.com

Contents

Introduction

How many cups of coffee have you had today? How many of them did you buy in a coffee shop?

The nine stories in Coffee: Hot are magical, even the ones that don't feature magic. Everything in here is about sex and coffee shops, two topics very dear to my heart. And, I'm sure, to yours. This anthology explores the sensual side of coffee shops. When you're in the coffee shop, you use all your senses. Everything is heightened. The glazed ceramic mug heats your hands, and you notice the way the warmth radiates. You raise the mug and taste the dark glory of your daily addiction. In the background, you hear the whir of steaming milk, smell the hot roasting beans.

Since the first coffee shop opened in 1475 Constantinople, coffee shop culture has wormed its way into society's functions. In the 1600s, coffee shops were the perfect places for drinkers to meet and do respectable business (and foment revolution). The caffeinated beverage and communal locations inspired academics and philosophers who worked faster and stayed sober longer. Now, they are hip standards on every corner. They are places for writers, homework-doers, and tentative daters.

These stories span the Victorian era through the space-faring future. They star real coffee beans... and some not so real. There are quiet tales with gods who sling espresso, and improbable stories like the one with the tentacle monster. (Yes! Tentacular coffee shop erotica! Who knew I needed it?) There's even an old-fashioned quest fantasy.

Bikini baristas wear tuxspeedos and serve the commuter crowd. Spies shelter in a coffee shop on a hostile planet, using their sensory-feedback tech for extracurricular purposes. Werecivets offer up life-changing supernatural coffee (think kopi luwak) to those with something worthwhile for barter. When humanity expands to the stars, illicit activities take root in places the coffee won't grow.

This anthology is for everyone who spends inordinate time and money in coffee shops (or only wants to, because few of these shops could really exist). Nine authors have come up with amazing tales of sexy, coffee-related drama. You will cackle over the cleverness and sigh over the quiet slices of life. At least, I did.

Intellectual. Social. Caffeinated.

Victoria Pond
Circlet Press
August 2015

The Great Coffee Machine
Axa Lee

The Great Coffee Machine was the phrase on everyone's lips. No one had seen it all assembled; they'd only seen the pieces of copper and steel as they'd been carried into the shop on Bond Street. Reportedly it was huge, running completely on steam power, though there had been some speculation as to the great switchboards and circuits that had also been seen entering the building on the backs of the workmen. The workers, if questioned, only shook their heads, and no amount of money could pry from their lips the secrets of the coffeehouse.

In the mornings, during the days before the opening, the neighborhood woke to a heavy fog lying over the city. But through that fog traveled the most alluring fragrance, the most exotic of scents, a smell that drew all the residents from their beds and out onto the streets, flocking onto the sidewalk in front of the shop, peering inward as inside the Great Machine bellowed and steamed.

The smell was coffee.

More precisely, it was the roasting beans and steaming brews the shop's proprietor ran through to be certain the machine was working. The smell alone had the whole neighborhood eager and peering, not to mention their curiosity regarding the machine within, as it pressed and burbled and hissed.

The only thing more speculated about than the machine itself was the owner.

"Blown into town like a leaf on the wind," some said.

"Floated in on a whiskey barrel blown off-course," said others.

"Abandoned by gypsies."

And indeed, the few glimpses of her around town revealed her to be as dark as a gypsy and as brightly dressed. She stood out in a town as drab as London, like her copper pipes, a gleaming spot of color in a city otherwise covered by fog, drizzle, or a thick coating of coal dust.

The day of the Grand Opening, the entire neighborhood lined up, eager for a look at the machine, half-desperate for a taste of what came from inside.

Like so many others about town, Alessandra Seymour had talked of nothing else for months.

"You shall put me off coffee altogether!" Nicholas, her long-time paramour had proclaimed.

"But shall you take me to the coffeehouse?" Alessandra had persisted. "You shall, shan't you?"

And after much pestering and twice as much badgering, cajoling, and downright bribery (of the womanly kind rather than the monetary, of course), there they stood in a long line along with every other curious bystander, eager to see the Great Machine, view the proprietor, and partake in the first female-friendly coffeehouse the city had ever seen.

Alessandra hung excitedly on Nicholas' arm, eagerly standing on her tiptoes, trying to see over the long line stretched out of the coffeehouse door and part way down the street.

"You're as fidgety as a flea," Nicholas complained and she apologized, trying to contain her eagerness. Nicholas smiled indulgently. "Imagine," he said. "A place that makes people wait, without regard to class." He glanced around them, making a point of lingering his attentions on the lower classes of people, the fishwives and the forge-mongers, in line with them, waiting for their morning cuppa.

She patted his arm.

"Don't be cross. The line is moving quickly, you see?" Indeed, they'd already moved almost to the door.

Coffeehouses had gone out of fashion years ago, but this was something new, something where all were included, and with the public house becoming a particular focus of the temperance people, the revival came at just the right time. Even if there was a wait.

"It better be worth it, that's all I'm saying," he gruffed. "And only because it's for you."

And then they were ducking through the door and Alessandra's eyes went wide.

The inside of the shop was all dark mahogany, with copper accents. It took a long time to take it all in, for even Alessandra's inquisitive mind to understand what she was seeing. What she had first supposed was decoration instead proved to be working pieces of the machine. And when she realized that, the full enormity of the thing amazed her. It occupied most of the shop, gargling and steaming. The thing was a great tangle of tubes and copper plating, running all the way up to the ceiling of the shop, filling the space there with a crushing amount of riveted machinery, pressuring chambers, big-bellied steam chambers, tubing and piping that spiraled around itself in complicated patterns before finally venting out the roof. Special holes had had to be cut, some reported, the old, narrow chimney proving inadequate. And Alessandra could see why: the thing must pull in and expel air at a prodigious rate. Great glass globes with rubber-coated pistons chuffed up and down, moving steam and a dark, smoky liquid through the exposed tubes, to be drawn into cups by the staff. It was truly a marvel to behold.

"What can I get you?"

The dark-haired woman wiped the counter with a bartender's towel and braced her hands against the glossy, finished wood.

Alessandra's wide-eyed gaze flicked to the blackboard hung on the wall behind the counter, traveling over the choices with the frantic terror of one who had no idea what she wanted. The colorful array of delicately swooping letters describing the drinks and their name might as well have been written in ancient Egyptian for all the sense Alessandra could make of it, mocha this and latte that, all as inscrutable as hieroglyphs.

The woman behind the gleaming mahogany counter smiled. Her eyes were dark as well, Alessandra noted, almost the same mocha as her hair. Her skin was the color of the Mediterranean, the kind that was light olive and tanned easily, leaving no blemishes. A prim little mouth slanted in a roguish smile. If chocolate had a smile, it would be that smile: tempting and lit from within by laughter.

"I can guess," the gypsy-dark beauty said. "I have somewhat of a reputation for guessing."

The proprietress, with her short bobbed hair and daring cut of her clothes, gave her a bold bearing and insolent smile, as if she knew a secret Alessandra couldn't bear anyone else to know. Alessandra couldn't place her accent, something between French and Portuguese—maybe Italian. The lyrical quality put her in mind of their time in Genoa, when Nicholas had installed her in a small villa located a short drive from his rented town house.

Beside her, Nicholas fidgeted.

"Guess," he grumped. "But by all that's holy let us sit. My sciatica."

His sciatica and pancreas had been acting up all week, a combination of too much rich food and drink and too much weight, gained from the aforementioned food and drink.

"Vienne, the press is stuck again," one of the counter assistants said.

The proprietress reeled off a list of orders and complicated mechanical tweaks that Alessandra couldn't follow, then turned back to her and Nicholas with a smile.

"Give me your hands." The proprietress extended her own hands, palms up, across the counter.

With a half-glance at Nicholas, Alessandra tentatively laid her hands palm-up, cupped by the long, warm fingers of the other woman. As Vienne's hands tightened around Alessandra's, a shiver of pleasure traveled up her arms and down her back, leaving goose-pimples in its wake. The alluring smells drifting from the coffee machine, the heat of the proprietress's hands, the days-long anticipation Alessandra had experienced, simply all combined so that in the moment their hands connected, the touch ignited something that torched its way across her skin and came to rest somewhere between her hip bones, her womanly parts becoming a vague ache of unmet desires.

Something stroked through Alessandra, something like a touch, but that left a tang on her tongue like sucking on copper pennies. It left her gasping, her skin raised and prickling. She looked up into Vienne's dark eyes, glimpsing something wild there for a moment, like catching a movement in the corner of your eye, where it's gone before its ever really there. She tasted violets then, and strawberries. And she sensed loneliness, so much loneliness and wanderlust that it was almost overwhelming.

Vienne jerked her hands away. Alessandra noted the flush up her neck, the rapid rise and fall of her chest.

"Interesting," Vienne murmured. She wiped her hands with the bartender's towel. Their eyes met as their hands parted and the vague ache turned sharp and insistent. "Café mocha. And steamed milk for him."

"Steamed milk..." Nicholas began, sounding affronted.

"Café au lait then." Vienne smiled, quickly appeasing him, but when she looked back at Alessandra her expression was less one of roguishness and more one of pensive inquisitiveness. "Take a seat and I'll bring it right out to you." With a wink at Alessandra, she vanished behind a panel at the side of the machine.

Alessandra turned back to Nicholas, who had ceased his complaining and studied her with much the same expression the proprietress had worn.

"What is it?" she asked. He waved her aside.

"Help me to the table over there." He gestured with his cane. "My gout." With no little effort, he heaved himself over to the table and seated himself with a groan. He set his hat on the table, leaned his cane against the wall beside him. He propped his offending leg out, though Alessandra judged it much the same as his other leg. Although she would never say so to him, she suspected his late wife had coddled his health, catering to his hypochondriac tendencies. It made him tough to manage at times, especially when he felt peevish. But even his peevishness could not detract from Alessandra's excitement about the coffeehouse.

All around them the establishment buzzed with voices, the clatter of crockery, not china, Alessandra noted, but thick, serviceable white cups, and heavy white plates beneath that doubled as saucer and plate. It was a stirring environment, one that sent a thrill through Alessandra's inners, though not as keen-edged a one as she'd experienced with the proprietress moments before. The heady, competing scents wrapped around her, eager for her attention, as the Great Coffee Machine heaved and guzzled in the background, adding a low hum of activity as it expelled steam, hissing dark as well as pale liquids from various copper spouts.

Alessandra became caught up in watching the machine work, in observing the identically clad counter assistants skitter to and fro, taking and filling orders, caffeinating what appeared to be most of London. Such an array of humanity entered the place! Alessandra had seldom seen such a spectacle of dukes and earls rubbing shoulders with carters and back alley whores. Some appeared quite put out and distressed by the lack of attention to rank, but their curiosity to see the Great Machine and taste its half-fabled concoctions overwhelmed their antiquated sense of propriety.

"First come, first serve," she heard the attendants say more than once when some upstart lord tried to jump the queue.

Vienne appeared at their elbows, startling Alessandra who had been thoroughly absorbed in the Duke of Coventry asking the fishwife next to him in line what she supposed the difference was between a mocha cappuccino and an espresso. Again, Alessandra felt that weight between her hip bones, as if something had settled there, constricting the air from her lungs at the same time to make her feel lightheaded.

"Thank you," she said to the proprietress. Their fingers brushed as Alessandra took her drink, the cup rattling discordantly against the saucer beneath, causing Nicholas to wince. His tinnitus, from years spent hunting with the baying of dogs and bugles.

"It's a marvelous machine, truly."

Vienne looked pleased with the compliment, but waved it off.

"Wherever did you find such a marvel?"

"I had it commissioned in Venice." She said it almost carelessly, her eyes frequently roving the shop, checking on both customer and server.

"It's beautiful."

That warm, chocolate smile made another appearance. "Thank you." Vienne laid her hand on Alessandra's arm, letting it linger a second longer than propriety dictated. Alessandra met her gaze and felt her insides turn molten at the heat she found there. Her mouth went dry and her heart suddenly beat light and fast in her chest.

"Well it's nice to have met you," she said. "But I have customers. If you need anything, just ask for me." She smiled again, a more professional courtesy this time.

Alessandra felt something bubble up within her, a desperation to keep Vienne there, if only for a few moments longer. She couldn't explain it, but the mysterious woman, the coffee machine, it made her desperate, desperate for more knowledge, for more time, almost frantically so, in a way she'd never experienced before. So she asked the first thing that popped into her head.

"Could you show me how it works?"

"Alessandra." Nicholas' rebuking tone made it sound as though he spoke to a child. "I'm sure the lady has much to do."

Alessandra dipped her head, abashed for having over-admitted her interest. Nicholas was a tolerant patron, but he sometimes grew weary and short with her questions.

"I find I am rather busy at the moment..." Vienne locked eyes with Alessandra, as though those clear brown eyes had the power to see straight into her mind. Her tone changed then, from business-like to almost flirtatious. "But if your lady would come back this evening, perhaps I could show the machine to her. Would that be acceptable?"

Although she spoke to Nicholas, her gaze never broke from Alessandra's.

Nicholas made a show of throat-clearing and huffing, but at last agreed, since Thursday nights he went to his Club.

"It's a date then," Vienne said. And with a quick air-kiss, she was gone.

"God's teeth," Nicholas said. "You're fair slicked up for that one en't ya?"

Startled, Alessandra set her cup down with a clatter.

Nicholas chuckled over her expression. "I know you better than that, darlin' girl," he said. He ran a finger over the exposed flesh of her bosom and neck. "I know that flush."

"No... I...."

Nicholas reached around to where she hid her hands in her lap to lay his large, meaty palm over hers. Her gaze met his.

"It's fine. Darlin' girl, I mean, I don't mind." He smiled, that gentle, loving smile she so treasured. "It's a woman, aye? I've given my blessing."

And he had. Alessandra remembered the conversation well. It had been shortly after he took her on as his mistress. He'd realized her keen affection for him as growing into something more than that. And he'd taken it upon himself to quash that tendency immediately.

"I won't be able to love you, you know."

She remembered him as he'd been, lying on his back on the bed, all but lost in the plush pile of pillows his money had bought for her. He liked her best like this, he'd told her, him lying back, with her skirts spread 'round them, concealing everything between them. Some men liked to watch, but not Nicholas. He liked to tell himself that she was, if common-born, still a lady in manner if not in reality. Early in their acquaintance he'd professed a particular liking to this position, as it put him in mind of his wife. That idea had touched Alessandra, as had the knowledge that his wife had been dead seven years at that time and he had not touched another woman since, nor been unfaithful to her during their some thirty years of marriage.

"If I can't have my wife, I'll take no wife at all." He'd declared this to her, simultaneously setting the exact expectations she could set regarding their relationship and disclosing vast layers of his character. He was a kind man, but one who preferred a professional relationship to a loving one now that his single marital relationship was over.

"My sons are older than you," he'd said. "So I'd ask you not to take other male lovers while we're together. I realize, however, that young women have needs. Should those needs arise I only ask that you sate them with a female lover. I've no desire to meet my son one day leaving the house of the mistress that I pay for. I ask only to know who else shares your bed. That doesn't mean anything else must change between us. So long as there are no other men."

"My lord, who could there be for me but you?" And she'd delivered the line and batted her eyes, making him chuckle with fondness.

But the need had arose, as Nicholas foretold, though Alessandra confined herself to the pleasure of her own self, rather than seeking out another sometimes-devotee of Sappho. It was simpler that way, and simple was the way they both wanted things.

Alessandra's gaze traveled to where Vienne gave a customer a skeptical look on an overly complicated order before handing them a simple cup of black coffee, before returning to Nicholas' placid, understanding expression. He was so caring, so considerate, so overwhelmingly understanding that, moved by his kindness, Alessandra reached up to cup his face affectionately.

"Really?" she asked.

He laid his hand over hers. "With that look on your face? How could any man say no?" With grave seriousness, he added, "I've told you before, I cannot love you. Not the way you deserve. If you can find that, you may pursue it, and with my blessing. I ask only to know who else shares your bed, nothing more."

Something inside of Alessandra softened and she kissed him impulsively on the opposite cheek.

He patted her hand.

"Now, my dear, I think it's time to go see about the medication for my rheumatism."

The coffeehouse was closed and only one light burned within

when Alessandra returned. She ordered Nicholas' driver to wait fifteen minutes for her and, if she did not return, to see himself home for the night. The smell of the coffee within made her bold as she applied her fist to the locked outer door. She had a speech all prepared for the minion coffee-server who would answer the knock, ordering them to see her to their mistress, but, to her astonishment, Vienne herself answered, wiping her hands on her ever-present bartender's towel.

"Well now," the coffee-maker said to the speechless courtesan. "I thought you might be back." She stood back from the door, allowing Alessandra to enter. She winked. "I'm a good guesser."

A bubble of laughter burst from Alessandra at seeing such a common gesture from such an uncommon woman, and she entered the dark coffeehouse.

The machine sat dormant, still a massive structure, imposing even in the dimness.

"Can you show me how it works?" Alessandra asked with a serious, earnest curiosity.

Vienne carefully smoothed the smile from her face and inclined her head. She led Alessandra behind the bar and to the heart of the machine, where all the levers and spouts sprouted from the copper and glass, spitting forth steaming hot brews at a touch. Vienne moved behind Alessandra to guide her hand over the levers. She explained each and every knob, every tube and ball and piston. Listening, Alessandra was keenly aware of her, of how she moved, of the brush of her hand, the twitches of muscle, of the way their words echoed in the space now that the machine stood quiet for the night. At last, Vienne fell silent, having explained all she could. Alessandra twisted her head back.

"It's beautiful," she said. "The design, it's...."

Vienne brushed a strand of hair off Alessandra's face. "Elegant," she finished. Her fingers lingered in Alessandra's hair. The younger girl blushed, feeling heat rise, a low-volume ringing in her ears. Breathlessness.

Vienne chuckled, as if sensing her reaction, and moved away. She went to a small stove in the corner. Dwarfed as it was by the monstrosity of the coffee machine, Alessandra hadn't noticed it before. Vienne stirred the fire and put a small saucepan on to boil.

"It's too late for coffee," Vienne explained. "But never for chocolate." She smiled and Alessandra found herself smiling back. She liked Vienne's smile, the way it made the fine creases at the corners of her eyes turn up, the mischief lurking in the background.

"Can you stir this," Vienne asked. "And keep stirring?"

Vienne stepped away from the stove. Alessandra continued to whisk the milk around the pan while Vienne arranged chairs around a small table.

"You enjoyed your coffee today?" Vienne asked.

"Very much," Alessandra said. "It was..." She searched for the word. "Luxuriant."

Vienne chuckled, a deep throaty sound that was both self-satisfied and amused, rich as the coffee itself.

"I'm glad. All of London is keen to see the machine, but don't know a thing about what the coffee should taste like." Her mouth twisted in a bitter smile. "I could serve them coffee made from whole beans soaked in hot water and still they would flock here for sheer novelty, at least for a while."

Vienne returned behind the bar and began measuring out powered substances into the heavy white cups. The milk on the stove began to bubble. She pulled it off and poured equal measures into both cups.

"Londoners are tricky," Alessandra said. "But you'll win them, in the end."

Vienne's gaze met hers, the coffee-colored gaze sharp and discerning.

"You think so?"

"Yes, I do. You're so...." Alessandra, blushing, stopped herself, looked away.

Vienne handed her a mug. Alessandra reached for it, but instead of the cup, Vienne took her hand, turning the unresisting palm up to inspect the lines. She was close enough Alessandra could smell the coffee on her skin, mixed with a scent like raw chocolate, her hair thick with the rich, smooth scent of dark grounds.

"Shall I guess your favorite?" the dusky madam asked. She trailed her fingers over Alessandra's palm, tipping her chin, casting her eyes upward; in what she must have known was an alluring look.

"I thought you did."

Vienne shook her head. "That wasn't your favorite."

"It wasn't?"

"But you know that. Out of all the things you want, dove, you enjoyed that coffee. Everyone enjoys my coffee. But that wasn't your favorite."

"But I don't want anything," Alessandra protested.

"Then why are you here, if that old man leaves you wanting for naught?"

Having no answer, Alessandra said nothing.

"Shall I tell you why you're here?"

Alessandra's skin prickled once more, her awareness of Vienne's proximity almost painful.

"You're here," Vienne continued, "because, deep down, you're curious. You want to know about things, to experience things, you crave it, in a way you've never craved your lover." She shot Alessandra another knowing glance. "Or maybe the way he's never craved you."

"He loved his wife," Alessandra finally said in a husky voice. "And he... we have an arrangement. A good one."

"Want. Need. Desire. You are so aware of everything, so keen to use all your senses. Yet you stay with him."

"He's kind to me."

"I'm sure."

"He gave me permission to be here." Alessandra wished the words back in mouth as soon as they escaped, but she persisted. "I won't leave him. I can't. But...."

"But you want something else as well?"

Alessandra nodded.

Vienne trailed her fingers over Alessandra's palm and wrist, eliciting the most delicious thrills over the younger woman's flesh.

"But you want more from him."

"I want what he cannot give me."

"You want to be craved, the way you crave; you want to be loved, and to love. You want to be kissed." Vienne stepped closer, narrowing the space between them. She cupped Alessandra's cheek. "As though you are the most precious thing in the world."

Alessandra's lips were quivering when Vienne's touched them. It was the softest, lightest of kisses, just a trailing of mouths, something fleeting, brittle, precious. She was still shaking when she opened her eyes and looked at Vienne's expressive, delicate face.

"And you?" Alessandra asked. "What's your favorite?"

Vienne leaned forward and kissed along Alessandra's collarbone and neck, making the other woman shudder and moan, arching into the caress.

She stood back from Alessandra for a moment. And both of them knew somehow that it was something greater than them both, that it was meant to be.

Vienne handed Alessandra the cooled mug of chocolate.

"Shall we sit?"

They did, and while Alessandra was glad of the reprieve, she still burned, craving Vienne to touch her again.

They spoke of mundane things, childhood and schooling. Alessandra found herself speaking often of Nicholas, the small, uncomplicated life she lived in the house he'd set up for her nearby.

"You're bored stiff," Vienne declared at last. "A mind like yours, curious about everything, you must be going mad."

"I read a lot."

Vienne set her mug down on the table with authority. "You must come here, every day; I'll teach you the machine. You could suggest improvements; keep it in good working order, that kind of thing."

Alessandra found herself smiling. "I'd like that," she said.

The linger. That breathless, impossible linger, between one breath and the next, the one Alessandra had learned in her profession to take advantage of. Yet in this circumstance she found herself unable to do it. She didn't want to see Vienne as a client, but as an equal, a lover. Perhaps even a friend.

Luckily Vienne had no such compunctions. She moved to the armchair so as to sit beside Alessandra. She took the cup from between Alessandra's hands and set it beside hers on the table, then turned back to her. Vienne traced Alessandra's jawline with the tips of her fingers, her gaze smoldering into the other woman's with a heat that lit Alessandra's insides with a low, steady flame. This want, this need, encompassed her, omnipresent, filtering through the entirety of her being, until the very roots of her hair felt alive to Vienne's touch.

"Kiss me," Alessandra wanted to beg. "Please kiss me."

But she didn't have to ask.

Vienne's lips were just as delicate this time, brushing over Alessandra's with a sure, gentle ferocity. Alessandra's flesh tingled, ready and straining for the touch of Vienne's hands. The kiss made Alessandra giddy, as though her head swam high-high-high above them, bobbing up somewhere in the sky with the kites the children flew in the park.

When she next became aware of herself, Vienne had pulled her across her lap. She had loosened Alessandra's corset, her hands massaging the generous flesh of Alessandra's bosom.

"Take off the dress," Vienne said next to her ear. Then bit the lobe.

Eager to please, Alessandra shed her heavy clothing and let Vienne tug her back down onto her lap.

"Come here," she said, and her tone made Alessandra shiver with pleasure.

Back to breast, she straddled Vienne's lap. Vienne's fingers trailed their way up the long length of Alessandra's thighs. Vienne parted her thighs, hand moving to the juncture of her legs to palm the entire vulva. She lingered there, pressing and exploring until

Alessandra grew breathless. The well-placed pressure made Alessandra moan and squirm with pleasure. Vienne brushed Alessandra's falling-down curls off of her neck, laying kisses along the skin there.

"You are so beautiful," she murmured. Alessandra bit her lip on a moan, instead reaching behind to grip Vienne, to stabilize herself.

Vienne pressed the heel of her hand against the rise of mons at the juncture of her pubic bones. Alessandra shuttered and moaned, fingers digging into Vienne's shoulder with her pleasure. Vienne began to stroke her, between her slick folds, teasing that to plumpness before expertly parting her flesh. Alessandra exclaimed, gripping Vienne's shoulders to keep her balance. Vienne's fingers moving in calculated rhythm, as she licked and kissed Alessandra's ear, neck, and back. Alessandra was gasping, lost in the rhythm of Vienne's fingers, working her clit, stretching inside her to press those hidden places that made Alessandra buck.

"That's it, dove, lean into me. Relax, let go." Vienne urged her along, all while pressing harder and deeper, stroking with increasing speed until Alessandra's hips shallowly pumped against her hand. "That's it, dove, yes, come for me."

Her pussy was slick, a puddle of juices, making wet noises as Vienne worked her fingers in and out of her. And her fingers pressed a certain way and Alessandra's world imploded, with a spasm of stars and a concussion of moons. Alessandra cried out as her orgasm broke over her and the tingles changed to electric shocks, spiking from her core to all over her body. She went limp, lying back in Vienne's arms, her cunt cupped by the coffee matron. Vienne kissed her ear.

Alessandra shuddered, reverberations of the encounter rolling through her. Vienne's lips were soft, delightfully so, delicate and yielding against her own.

"Keep me," Alessandra wanted to ask.

When she regained control of her legs, she allowed Vienne to guide her down the hall to her room. Once there, they made an unhurried exploration of one another. A slow stripping of clothing, a layering of kisses over trembling flesh, frequent deep-eyed gazing and deep, lingering kisses. Alessandra's limbs felt weighted, bloated, yet ready to float from the bed. Indeed, her head felt barely tied to her shoulders, bobbing somewhere over them, as if it was all an out-of-body experience. Vienne's hands were magic, and her mouth was bliss, and when she laid both upon her body, Alessandra couldn't imagine ever wanting to be anywhere else.

Vienne's dark head traveled down the pale contours of Alessandra's body, lips brushing over the sensitive sides of her breasts before moving inward to seize the nipple between her teeth, licking and sucking until the flesh hardened, which wasn't long at all since the chill in the air of the night-filled shop licked eagerly over Alessandra's skin. She shivered and Vienne smiled.

"If it's a chill you feel, dove, let me warm you."

And Vienne straddled her, kissing down along her neck and across her chest. Vienne kissed her way down Alessandra's body, pausing in all the right places to make the young miss writhe, tossing her head side to side on the pillow. Her fingers were once again buried in Alessandra's slit, working rapidly to bring her to fruition. Breathless, Alessandra urged her onward, not to stop, riding Vienne's hand and face with a ferocity that almost frightened her. And then she was coming, the great wave breaking over her, a thousand bolts of lightning flickering all over her body at once, her clit and slit feeling well-fucked and engorged beyond recognition as the residual spasms rode their way through her and passed away.

Vienne collapsed beside her, her lips shiny and smelling of pussy.

"I'm sorry..." Alessandra started to say.

"No," Vienne said. "No. Don't you dare." And Alessandra kissed her, tasting her own essence on the other woman's lips and privately thinking it tasted divine.

Later, they lay talking. It turned to Nicholas.

"I am his whore," she said of Nicholas. "And while I might

love him, I am not his lover. He's made that very clear, that she is dead, and that ours is a business arrangement."

"You love him," Vienne said softly.

"Of course I do." Alessandra rubbed her hands up and down the smooth skin of her lover's body, reveling in the sleek softness of her. "He loved his wife, he told me that. She was his only love. He's fond of me, but his love is dead and I am there to fuck him, to care for him, to be on his arm at the opera." She wiped tears from the corners of her eyes, careful to dab so as to not smear her kohl, then kissed Vienne's hair. "But he does not mind me seeking that out in others."

Vienne watched Alessandra, her look inscrutable but not unkind as her fingers traced over Alessandra's body.

Alessandra sniffed, then reached up, brushing back fallen strands of Vienne's hair.

"But you have a story too, I think."

"My story is long, and begins a very long way from here." Vienne slowly traced her fingers over Alessandra's nipples, light, deft strokes, until the flesh tightened, pressing up against her fingertips. "I was blown in on a west wind, left my own people. Some call me a witch, others...." She shrugged. "A clever woman from Genoa." Vienne smiled over Alessandra's soft sighs. "Either way, it doesn't matter what I am. I'm here. You're here. My story," Vienne said, sitting up and kissing her way up Alessandra's body. Alessandra shivered beneath Vienne's touch. "Is that you intrigue me. And not very many people intrigue me."

She reached Alessandra's mouth, who laughed and kissed her, arms going around the other woman's shoulders.

Vienne leaned up on an elbow, the two of them looking into one another's eyes.

"I am not the jealous kind," she said. She touched Alessandra's hair. "As long as he shares as well as I do, he may have your keeping, your body, your heart. So long as you will also share as much with me."

"Yes," Alessandra promised. "Yes. Everything."

And they fell into one another's arms again, rocking together with a quiet, ecstatic ferocity.

In the morning, a once-again dressed and well-fucked Alessandra walked out of the coffeehouse at dawn. The street lights were lit, but dawn was slowly rising as she made her way through the fog, her thoughts with both of her lovers, their happy arrangement, and the new job she would start next Thursday: learning the Great Machine from beginning to end. The idea thrilled her, even more deeply than did the thought of working beside Vienne. Nicholas would shake his head but smile behind his morning paper and let her do as she would, the same as he had always done. She kept him young, and though he said he didn't love her, she knew he retained a fondness for her zest and curiosity. It kept him from thinking overmuch of only himself. With a smile, Alessandra walked faster, eager to tell him about her night, the scent of coffee trailing through the neighborhood at her heels.

Dark Roast
Justin Josh

"You've been holding out on me," I said angrily.

Becker Mack opened the door to his cabin and motioned for me to sit down. "Carlos," he said. "Thanks for coming. You're not going to believe what I've got for you."

"Coffee," I said. "I can smell it." I couldn't believe it. I hadn't tasted coffee in nearly two years. It was impossible that he had hoarded it this long. Not on this crowded spaceship way out here in the middle of nowhere.

"You can smell that?" he asked, surprised.

"Smells freshly brewed," I said. I had always been blessed with a superior sense of smell. Unfortunately, onboard ship it was more of a curse. "French roast?"

"Not exactly," he said, opening a thermos and pouring me a cup. "Go ahead, try it."

I reached for the cup and stopped. "Wait," I said. "What's the catch? What's this going to cost me?"

Mack spread his hands innocently. "It's free. No catch."

I narrowed my eyes at him. It wasn't like Mack to just give things away. There had to be a catch. And yet, the coffee smelled damn good. Against my better judgment, I grabbed the cup and took a sip.

Heaven! The rich aroma wafted into my nostrils as the hot liquid poured onto my tongue. My taste buds exploded in flavor. I groaned involuntarily. It had been so long.

Mack laughed. "You like it?"

I trembled as I took another sip. "What the hell is in this?" There was an exotic spicy tang to it that I couldn't identify. Already I could feel the effects of the coffee pulsing through my veins.

"Not bad, eh?"

"It's fantastic," I said. "Where'd you get it?"

"It's a secret," said Mack, lowering his eyebrows. "I can't tell you."

"What's the deal, Becker?" I asked. "Why are you being so nice to me? You never give anything away for free. What do you want?"

He shook his head. "You got it all wrong. I don't want anything from you."

He was lying. Mack's voice always raised an octave when he lied, which was how I was able to beat him at our weekend poker games.

"Fine," I said. "Don't tell me." I took another sip of the coffee.

The next day found me banging on his cabin door. I was trembling and sweaty and nauseous. It was the damn coffee. I needed another cup and I needed it now. If I didn't get that coffee soon, I was going to explode. One cup and I was addicted, a complete junky.

Mack opened the door.

"Damn you!" I said, plopping myself into a chair. "I knew there was a catch. You put some kind of drug in the coffee and now you've gotten me addicted. Damn you. Get me another cup. I'll pay anything."

"Slow down," said Mack, chuckling innocently. "I didn't put anything in your coffee."

"The hell you didn't!" I roared. "Come on. Quit stalling and give me a cup. How much will it cost me?"

"I don't have any here," he said. "But if you meet me down in animal husbandry in an hour I can set you up."

"Fine," I said.

"We'll discuss the terms when you get there," he said.

"I knew it!" I snarled. "Free, my ass!"

"Hey, the first cup was free," Becker said.

"Wait," I said. "Why down in animal husbandry?" I asked suspiciously. I knew that Becker worked down there. Maybe that's where he was hiding his stash.

"You'll see," he said. "Meet me in one hour."

"I ought to report you to the captain."

"Go ahead," said Mack. "But if you do, don't expect to get any more of your precious coffee." He bounced his eyebrows triumphantly.

It was the longest hour in my life. Heart pounding and palms sweaty, I climbed down into the bowels of the ship to the animal husbandry section. As soon as I entered, the dank mustiness from all the alien animals assaulted my nostrils. Each of them had been taken from a planet we had visited. Now they were being shipped back to Earth.

I tried not to look at them snorting and stomping in their stalls. I had never really been an animal person. And I was definitely not an alien animal person. Still I couldn't help but notice the variety of odd creatures: giant hairy spider-like things the size of sheep, weird snakey animals with multiple heads, a beast which looked like a cross between a cockroach and a rat. They chittered and whickered and snorted, making all kinds of odd sounds that set my teeth on edge.

A few workers gave me strange knowing glances. They knew why I was there, I realized. I didn't care. I needed that coffee.

I found Mack standing in the back, next to one of the large stalls. "You came," he said, with false surprise.

"Quit the small talk," I said angrily. "Where's my coffee?"

"You're going to have to pay," said Mack.

"Fine. How much?" I pulled out my credit-chip.

"Not money," said Mack, pointing to the stall. "Something else."

I looked in the stall. Inside was a giant alien creature. It looked like a cross between an octopus and a centipede. It was about the size of a whale and was covered with all kinds of grotesque protrusions and boils and crevasses, several of which were oozing dark liquid. It also had hundreds upon hundreds of tentacles of all shapes and sizes, short ones, long ones, thin ones and thick ones. Of all the creatures there, this was easily the largest and most grotesque.

Then I smelled it: the distinct aroma of roasted brew. It was coming from one of the nipple-like protrusions. Suddenly I realized where Mack had gotten the coffee. My stomach turned.

At the same time, my cravings doubled. I wanted to rush into the stall and fix my mouth on one of the creature's leaking boils.

"You bastard," I said.

"It's called a gorlon," said Mack. "And if I were you, I'd be nice to it. It has the coffee you are craving so badly."

"Coffee, huh?"

Mack shrugged and grinned guiltily. "I never actually said it was coffee. You just assumed."

"Just tell me the price," I said.

Mack looked at me levelly. "You're not going to like it," he said.

"I'm celebrating already," I said. "Just tell me."

He tilted his head at the gorlon, which was now writhing several of its tentacles excitedly. "He likes humans," said Mack. "If you know what I mean." He winked.

I stared at the creature nervously. "No," I said, afraid at what Mack was implying. "What are you saying?"

"You know...." Mack gestured at my body, eyeing me up and down.

I gulped. "You mean?" I couldn't say it. Hell, I couldn't even imagine it.

"Sorry," said Mack. "That's the price. Take it or leave it." He smiled dryly.

I wanted nothing more than to knock that sneer off his face. Yet at the same time, those damn cravings were getting stronger. I wasn't sure I could resist them any longer. Why was Becker doing this to me?

I looked over at the gorlon, my eyes settling on one of the leaking boils. As if noticing my stare, the gorlon squirted the nipple, sending an arc of glistening liquid to my feet. The aroma of freshly brewed dark roast rose upward. I trembled. How bad, I wondered, could it be? It wouldn't take that long. Why not?

"What exactly do I have to do?" I asked.

Mack grinned widely and folded his arms across his chest. "I knew you'd come around. Don't worry. It won't hurt you. You might actually like it. Just go inside. It will do the rest."

"What's it going to do me?" I asked nervously.

"It just wants to have some fun," said Mack. "You'll see. Go on. It's waiting."

It squirted more coffee at me. That was it. I was ready. I began to take off my clothes.

Mack stopped me. "Don't," he said. "It likes to undress you. Just go inside." He opened the door to the stall.

"You're not going to watch are you?" I asked, feeling suddenly shy. I couldn't believe I was doing this.

"You won't even notice me," said Mack, pushing me gently into the stall. "Trust me."

"Trust you?" I snorted, stumbling forward.

Mack was right. I forgot about him completely. The gorlon quickly captured my full attention when four long tentacles whipped out and curled around my wrists and ankles.

It pulled me into a tight spread-eagled position and lifted me up off the ground. It was so strong! I couldn't move. My heart thumped wildly. What had I gotten myself into?

I yelped in fear as the tentacles wound up and pulled me closer. It dangled me in the air as several smaller tentacles reached out and began to slowly undress me.

I marveled at its gentle dexterity. While one pair of tentacles fiddled with my belt and pants, another began to pull off my boots. At the same time, yet another pair of tentacles began to unbutton and remove my jacket. Instead of being repulsed, I felt a thrill of energy run through me. Its grip on me was so strong. I could feel the warm coils pressing against my flesh. Its touch was surprisingly sensual—so delicate and playful. Goosebumps rippled across my skin.

After it removed my boots, it shucked off my pants. Seconds later my jacket and shirt were pulled off. I was now held spread-eagled next to it dressed in nothing but my underwear. The cool air of the room prickled my skin. I started breathing heavily. I had to admit, there was something about the way it held me in such a vulnerable position that was turning me on. Oh, crap! I was getting hard!

Only then did I see the row of dark eyes on the top part of the gorlon's body. All its eyes stared at me. I felt so naked in front of it. I looked over at Becker and saw him standing outside the stall. He was holding something up in his hand. Damn him! Was he filming this?

The gorlon pulled my gaze back as a series of smaller tentacles extruded from its body and began to caress my chest, my abs, my inner thighs, my arms. Soon it was caressing me over my entire body. I shivered under its delicate touch. No lover had ever been so careful or attentive. So tender and soft, while at the same time, sparkling and crackling with electricity. It was playful and yet so assertive and dominant.

This was fantastic. I moaned with pleasure. The gorlon seemed to be able to read my mind. It knew exactly where to touch me to turn me into a quivering helpless man.

I gasped and moaned involuntarily as more tentacles came out and tore off my underwear.

I looked down and saw that I had a full erection. Another tentacle reached out and began to curl around the base of my shaft, gripping it tightly. Yet another tentacle flicked out and curled around my ball sack, pulling it down gently.

I whimpered with pleasure and my entire body thrashed and spasmed. I was nothing more than a puppet. My body was no longer my own. And I was loving it.

The gorlon continued to service my body. It stroked my cock more vigorously. I felt intense pleasure from my nipples and saw that it had fixed the tips of two tentacles to each nipple and was sucking and nibbling at them. I could feel soft tongues flicking in and out. I arched my back and thrust my chest forward. It felt so good!

I sensed other tentacles softly grasping my earlobes. Oh, it was also kissing my neck. Goose-bumps covered my skin as waves of bliss pulsed through my body. Was that me making that moaning sound? Every move it made sent me into another paroxysm of ecstasy.

Suddenly I felt it envelope my cock. I looked down and saw

that it had pulled my erection inside one of its crevasses, which was now clamping tightly on my shaft. I could feel several tongues licking and sucking me.

I heard myself screaming loudly with pleasure as it took one long thin tentacle and began to work its way between my butt cheeks.

"Oh! Oh!" I screamed weakly as it entered inside me. It then began to move in and out, exploring my ass.

My entire body exploded with pleasure. I screamed, yelped, roared, groaned, moaned. The gorlon was merciless. Whatever this creature was, it knew precisely how to pleasure a man's body.

I had had plenty of sex in my days, but never anything like this. Just when I thought it couldn't feel any better, the gorlon began to caress the insides of my thighs, then tickle my armpits. Oh, I was so close!

It began to lightly spank my ass. I trembled with ecstasy. The pleasure was getting stronger and stronger. I needed a release! But it was in total control. When would it let me come?

Suddenly it maneuvered me slightly and I felt a tentacle enter my mouth. No, it was one of the boils. It was squirting coffee down my throat. I guzzled the liquid gratefully. It coursed through entire body, heightening my already dizzying state of bliss.

At the same time, the gorlon began to work my body even harder. I could feel it fucking my ass back and forth, while two tentacles held my hips, rocking them. It kept my cock tightly gripped in its lips, bringing me right to the brink of climax and keeping me captive there.

Sweat covered my body and I gasped for air. So this was what sex was like. Everything before was a pale comparison. I wanted only to be pleasured by this massive beast. It was my now my master. Nothing else mattered.

Then I saw something I couldn't believe. It was Becker Mack. He had entered the stall and was—like me—being taken by the gorlon. I watched as Mack's clothes were teased from his body and flung to the side. Various tentacles wrapped around him.

He too began to groan with pleasure. While I was somewhat distracted by my own situation, I couldn't help but notice that Mack was also pulled so that he was spread-eagled, buck naked and pierced by the creature. It clearly knew what it liked. And seeing Mack's smile and sizeable erection, I knew he was liking it too. I wasn't surprised. He had no choice. The gorlon was incredibly talented.

It had no mercy. It fucked us both for what felt like hours. I climaxed at least three times, maybe more. And judging by Mack's screams, so did he.

Still the gorlon wouldn't release us.

I was nearly unconscious as it observed me with its many eyes. I had the distinct feeling it was smiling at me.

And then it released me. I fell to the floor of the stall and gasped for air, trying to regain my strength. Mack, I saw, was already jumping up and moving around.

"Quickly," he said, pointing a few small buckets along the edge of the stall. "We don't have much time."

I looked up blearily and saw that the gorlon was kindly squirting out several streams of its precious coffee. Mack held two buckets, trying to capture as much as he could. "Hurry!" he repeated.

He didn't have to tell me twice. Still naked and in an afterglow haze, I crawled over, grabbed two buckets and held them under the now dwindling streams. Unfortunately I was only able to get a small amount before the streams ended.

"Come on," said Mack. "Follow me." He carried the buckets out of the stall.

"Grab our clothes," he said.

I looked around and began to run back and forth. Our clothes were strewn widely and I had to avoid the gorlon's twisting tentacles. It occasionally reached out and teased me, tickling my neck, slapping my naked ass, or curling around my waist.

I was incredibly relieved when I finally exited the stall and Mack slammed the door shut.

We both leaned against the wall and looked at each other with knowing glances. We were both thinking the same thing. We were slaves to the gorlon. Nothing else mattered but having sex with it and drinking its precious nectar.

"How long have you known about this?" I asked, throwing him his clothes and getting dressed.

He also got dressed and began to store the coffee we had collected. "You're not going to like it."

"Why start now," I said. "Just tell me."

Mack leaned against the wall. "Well, it's like this. I was assigned to take care of the gorlon right after it came on board, see. I was the one who fed it and cleaned its stall. It wasn't long before I learned of its ability to make coffee. I tried it and what can I say? I liked it."

"You mean it got you addicted," I said.

He shrugged. "I soon learned that it had certain preferences. So we kind of worked out an arrangement. I give it guys to play with, and it keeps me supplied with fresh java."

I felt sick to my stomach. "You pimped me out! For coffee!"

"Hey, don't blame me. You chose to come here. Besides, I saw everything. You enjoyed it."

Suddenly I remembered him taking pictures. "Did you record the gorlon and me?" I asked.

He flashed an oily grin. "Only for a few minutes. Just in case you decide to rat me out."

"I can't believe you!" I said. "Just give me my coffee, you bastard. I'm going and never coming back."

"Take it," said Becker, handing me my half. "But you'll be back. Everyone always comes back."

"How many others?" I asked.

Mack looked at me hesitantly. "A few."

"A few? How many is a few?"

"Never mind," he said. "You've got your fix. Now get out of here."

"This isn't over," I said. I held the thermos against my chest and stalked away.

I couldn't believe it. That damn gorlon was taking over our ship. Right under our noses, one by one, we were becoming addicted. All because Mack Becker had to have his coffee.

Against my better judgment, I went to go see Captain Contreras.

"What's this about?" he said, looking at me sternly from across the table.

We were in the brig interrogation room. Nothing but a table and two chairs, and of course, security cameras. I should have known this would be recorded. Outside two security men guarded the door. This could go badly for me.

I coughed. Perhaps this was a mistake. Now that I was here, I realized how bizarre my story sounded. I closed my eyes and took a deep breath. I had to do what was right. Even now the odor of the gorlon-coffee lingered in my nostrils. I couldn't escape it. "Captain," I said. "I believe that there are illegal activities occurring on the ship."

Captain Contreras leaned back in his chair and looked at me with an expression of amusement. "You do?" he asked.

"Yes, sir. I know this going to sound strange, but you've got to believe me. It's a long story. It all began several days ago when I thought I smelled—"

"Wait," said the captain, holding up his hand. He reached behind his desk, lifted up a pitcher and proceeded to pour two cups of a steaming dark liquid. "Before you start, let's both lean back and have a cup of freshly brewed coffee. My treat," he said, smiling.

...And Friday is Formal Day
Owen James Franks

My alarm goes off at 4am, like normal. I shower, dress, grab a muffin, throw a raincoat over my work attire, grab my backpack, make sure that both deadbolts in my crap-hole apartment are locked, and hop in my car for the 15-minute drive to open Firehouse Beans, the coffee stand I work at.

I unlock the stand and wave to Amber as she's doing the same thing at my "competition" across the highway. No raincoat for her, she just doesn't seem to care about even a hint of modesty. She's got sparkly red horns, small, feathery wings that look way too expensive for a cheap Halloween costume, a tiny red bikini top and bottoms, and red thigh-high boots. She's brought out her favorite devil costume for Fabulous Friday again. Not that she needs that as an excuse or anything. I mean hell, the name of the stand she works at is Sexy Devils' Coffee.

Amber and I have chatted a few times outside of work. She's hot, if you like blondes with big tits, which most of her customers apparently do. Mostly we've compared customer breakdowns. The funny thing is, we mostly get the same kinds of people, just flip the genders. She gets more pushy frat boys asking for inappropriate things, I get more pushy cougars who got where they are in life by never taking no for an answer.

Okay, there are a few differences. I've never had patrons yell at me to show my tits, or been offered twenty bucks to lick whipped cream off another barista. Not that I wouldn't happily do that to Amber for free, amongst other things, but we never really hit it off like that. When part of your job is flirting with the customers, sometimes you just want to turn it off once you leave the job, and it's nice to just be able to talk to someone who understands what your day is like.

I'm in at 4:50. Ten minutes gives me enough time to get cups, beans, flavors, and all the other things I need ready to go for my first customers, and hang my raincoat on a peg behind the tiny washroom door. Check the mirror, straighten my bow-tie, make sure my tux-speedo isn't showing off anything I don't want to, and flip on the Open sign. Oh, and take a selfie to post to the stand's Instagram account. Formal Friday is usually good for a few new followers, and the occasional curious new customer.

My first customers arrive just a couple minutes after the stand is open. It starts as a trickle, mostly career women heading into work early, and wanting a little side of beefcake to hand them their morning latté. I smile, make cheerful conversation about the weather about twenty times an hour, and rake in some decent tips. Across the way, Amber is doing the same thing for her mostly male customers.

The commute rush starts to taper off around 8am, to be replaced by the school drop-off crowd. I'm always glad when summer vacation is over, because a lot of my best tippers are bored soccer-moms who've just dropped two or three kids off at school and want a taste of fantasy or hint of danger, plus a triple-soy caramel macchiato, before they head home for the morning. Amber gets her share of soccer dads too, but not nearly as many. Then again, she's busier during the peak commute time, so I guess it evens out.

By 10am, I can finally catch my breath. The cars slow to a just a few per hour, and I can start cleaning up and getting the stand ready for the afternoon guy. Except, dammit, that flaky twerp just texted me that he's "sick" and not coming in. I'll just bet he's sick. Not that I'll complain too much about picking up extra hours, but something tells me Gabby, the stand's owner, is going to be hiring again soon, especially since I have to message her that I'll be closing tonight, and not Blake.

This is the slow time for both my stand and Sexy Devils across the road. Just the occasional car rolling through, usually someone with a day off from work, or else just passing through and curious about the whole "bikini barista" scene that we have in the

Northwest. Of course the curious ones are usually over at Amber's window, but I get the occasional dude who either made a really embarrassing mistake, or completely not a mistake at all.

I have a few regulars who swing by too. Most of these I know by name, and half the time, have a drink ready for them before the car even rolls up. There's always a few customers trying to get my attention, and I'm happy to encourage a little flirting. It's not for nothing that my tip jar says "Just the tip" on it.

I take a break at one, throw my raincoat on, and walk around the outside of the stand. Just making sure that no one's thrown a bag of trash where I can't see it, missed the tip jar and dropped money on the ground, or whatever. Amber's got a customer again, two dudes in a lifted bro-dozer pickup truck.

I pause and take a closer look at the truck. Amber mentioned before that for some reason, guys with big, lifted pick-ups seem to be the ones most likely to cause her problems, and judging by what I can see through her window, this one takes the cake. Her arms are moving, she looks like she's yelling, and I'm pretty sure her face is turning an alarming shade of red. Whatever Bubba asked her to do, she's not happy, and he's not backing down.

That's when the pistol comes out the driver's window of the truck. I do a double-take, and realize that Bro #2 has a gun as well, and that they're both pointed in Amber's direction. I'm as far from the door to my stand as I can get, and the flat crack of several pistol shots reaches my ears before I can even get back inside. I'm fumbling to pull my phone out of my bag when I hear more shots, much louder this time, like somebody opened up with a shotgun or something.

My phone is finally out of my bag, but as I'm fumbling to punch my unlock code, there's a final, massive explosion, followed by a pair of smaller, secondary explosions. I yank open one of the stand's side windows, and it's nothing but chaos. The bro-dozer is a smoking wreck. Sexy Devils looks like the Big Bad Wolf blew over a house of sticks. Whatever those assholes were trying to do, I'm pretty sure that wasn't it.

I don't remember when I went back out the door and started to cross the street. Lucky for me traffic basically disappears in the early afternoon, because all I can think about is whether Amber's somehow alive. I can't imagine how she could be, but I have to check anyway.

The stand just looks like a giant pile of toothpicks. I'm not even sure where to start, when I see movement. There's no way it could be, and yet, that movement is followed a few seconds later by bright red painted nails, a hand, then an arm, and then somehow, impossibly, Amber just sort of pulls herself out of the rubble.

Her bikini top and bottoms are nothing but charred, tattered fabric, and she brushes them off like they weren't even there. Her devil horns and wings have somehow come through unscathed, and she glances around, flips the bird at the truck, and yells at what's left of her visitors.

That's when she sees me, with my jaw drooping to the ground, and my raincoat untied and flapping in the slight breeze. She smiles, and once again, I don't remember crossing the road back to my stand. I can't help but notice that not only is there not a single burn mark on her body, but she's even more gorgeous naked than I imagined. I should have tried harder to ask her out before. I don't know how those wings are staying in place without any straps, and I don't really care.

Once we're inside my stand, I try to offer her my raincoat, which she ignores and perches herself on the edge of the counter, smiling all the while. "I knew having this stand as a backup was a good idea." She says, more to herself, it seems, than to me.

"What?" is the only thing I can think to say.

She finally looks at me, eyes focusing on my face for maybe the first time. "Hmm, well, you're not screaming or calling the cops yet. That's a good sign. All right, stud, you get three questions. Make them count, so I can decide what to do next."

I'm still not sure my brain's working right. Did I just hear the woman who somehow walked away unscathed from a massive explosion tell me that I had three questions to help her decide what to do? I guess I did. Okay, I need to make these good, preferably without getting too distracted by the phenomenal body that she's unabashedly putting on display.

"Um, okay. How the explosion? Why you okay? What you mean having this stand?"

She raps on my head, gently, with the knuckles of her perfectly manicured left hand. "I hope that you're just still in a bit of shock, and you don't actually talk like a caveman all the time. Although, those guys were hung! Terrible conversationalists though. Couldn't make coffee worth a damn, but I suppose we didn't have coffee back then either. Or fire, for a while. Oh, right, your questions. What the hell, since you've handled things well so far, I'll tell you the truth.

"Home-boys in the truck turned out to be demon hunters. We were having a mildly animated conversation about my right to a continued existence, then they went and pulled those guns on me. So I blew up their truck and got the stand as collateral damage. Oopsy. Good thing I'm nigh immortal. It takes more than 9mm bullets and some C4 to scratch this lovely hide."

She takes a minute to breathe, and ticks down two fingers on her left hand. Her right hand's off doing something too, but I'm for some reason, I'm too pre-occupied to care about anything beyond what she's saying.

"So that's one, which dovetails nicely into two, namely, that I'm an immortal Succubus. Close your mouth, stud, you're drooling.

"And for your third question. I own this stand. And that one. Because it turns out that harnessing the lust of a few hundred coffee drinkers a day is a much simpler way to get what I need than actually seducing people. Well, usually. Except that having to walk away from an explosion really takes a lot of energy out of a girl. And I'm going to be down a stand for a while. What's a girl to do?"

I think there was a question in there somewhere, but I'm not really sure. I can't seem to focus on anything beyond her, and how I want her more than I've wanted a woman in my entire life.

"Oh, that's right, it's less of a what than a who." She tilts her head to the left a little bit, like she's sorting through some ideas. "Oh, that's a good one! Let's start with that." She practically purrs the last bit, and I have a vague sense that the blinds have been closed and the Open signed turned off before she grabs a can of whipped cream and squirts a big dollop over each round, full breast.

"Better lick that off, stud. You're going to need some energy."

I do as I'm told. As I finish with the left side, she sprays another line down to her belly-button. I lick that too, but when I start to go farther down, she pulls me back up again, and twists my arms behind my back. It's a motion that pulls us together, and my erection pushes up against her naked pelvis through my speedo.

She tilts her head towards my ear and whispers: "Not yet, stud. I like to be in control. Beg a little first."

"Please," escapes my lips.

"Please, what?" she whispers, and bites my ear softly.

"Please, mistress?" I whisper.

"Better. Now, lose the formal wear."

I start to loosen my bow-tie. She grabs my hands again. "Not that. You can keep that, but the tux has to go."

My briefs hit the floor faster than I can even think to push them down. She grabs me by the bow-tie and leans back against the wall, little red wings flattening out on either side as she pulls me towards her. She's warm, and her skin is the softest I've ever felt. I kiss her mouth deeply, hungrily, tasting her and the whipped cream. I gently fondle one of her breasts with my right hand, and slip my left hand lower, reaching behind her to cup her ass and pull us closer.

My left hand moves up, caressing her lower back before reaching the roots of her wings. They're soft, not feathery, but downy, and she moans as I rub the base of one.

She pushes me away again and drops to her knees to take my erection into her mouth. She licks up one side and down the other, then gently bobs the head in and out of her mouth. She runs one fingernail up the shaft with agonizing slowness, grinning wickedly as she does. "Oh, yes, you'll do nicely. Work's got you all pent up, doesn't it? All that flirting, but nothing to spend it on. Poor stud, someone should give you a raise."

"But you're going to have to earn it, first," she says as she moves to sit delicately in the only chair in the stand. She still has the whipped cream canister in one hand, and now she sprays around her shaved mound. "All right stud, I gave you a tease, now it's your turn. On your knees, and eat."

I obey almost before the words can register. It's sweet cream, then salty skin as I gently lick around her sex, then up, softly caressing her with my tongue. I slip a couple of fingers inside her wetness as she moans softly. "That's right, more of that, right there."

She pushes my head into her, as I keep licking and sucking where she likes it most. I keep my right hand moving in and out, and she moans again, louder. I can feel her thighs starting to tremble a little bit with every lick, and I slow down, drawing out the moment until she releases. She shudders, and I want nothing more than to be inside her. She knows it, sliding off the chair and pushing me down onto the floor, then straddling my hips, just above where I desperately want her to be.

She smiles. "Good boy. I think you're going to work out well. Now, what do you have left?" I'm already so aroused, I shudder just from her touch as she glides back on me, before levering herself up to slip my cock inside her. My hands come up around her hips, gently rocking her back and forth while she slips one hand down for herself.

We rock together, me guiding her on me for a few moments before she grabs my hands and pulls me up. Half-seated now, she pushes my hands behind her and onto her wings, sighing in ecstasy as I rub the sensitive bases where they meld into her back. "Oh, gods, I haven't been able to use this form for centuries. Right there!" My hands slide up and down her back as she rides me to completion. A wave builds up inside of me and I can do nothing but release it inside of her, gasping as her body shudders in time with mine as I empty a wave, no an ocean, into her.

I'm spent. Drained. More than I've ever felt before.

She smiles, suddenly gentle as she pushes off of me, and helps me to my feet. Now she wraps my raincoat around herself. "You know, I'm not sure how your boss is going to feel about you fucking the competition on the job." There's a wicked grin on her face as she continues. "Oh that's right, I'm your boss. I guess that means you get away with it, this time. In fact, I might even give you a raise. That energy you just provided ought to keep me going until I can get Sexy Devils up and running again."

Her features suddenly change. The horns and wings disappear, the blonde hair changes to brunette, and it's not Amber standing in front of me now, but my boss and stand owner, Gabby. "I'll save you the question. Shapeshifter too. Makes hiring easier. And from what I hear, I've gotta get another afternoon side of beefcake in here, plus go see some boring insurance men about the gas leak that tragically destroyed my coffee stand. Lucky for me I had stepped out for a few minutes to get some supplies."

She slaps my ass, and turns around to walk out the door. "Better get re-opened. Oh, and don't forget to put your tux back on. I run a classy establishment, not some sleazy joint where you can serve coffee with your dick hanging out."

And then she's gone, leaving me to try and get ready for the afternoon crowd with legs still wobbling from the most intense sex I've ever enjoyed. It's back to moms on their way to pick up the kids from school, afternoon commuters, and finally closing up. None of them knows how their hungry eyes are feeding a creature who stepped straight out of a myth. I'm never going to look at this job the same again.

His Name Was Pumpkin Spice
Greer Thompson

He was wiping down the counters when there was a pounding on the door, rattling the frame. Turner looked up from behind the order counter, blowing his dirty blonde bangs out of the way to get a clear view. A man, silhouetted by streetlights, stood at the door of the coffee shop, dripping wet from the rain that pounded down outside. Turner set down the rag and got out his keys, unlocking the door from the inside. The man pushed himself inside as soon as the door was open, and Turner shoved the door closed behind him and locked it up again.

Turner looked him up and down. The man was about six feet tall, brawny and dark-skinned with jet-black short-cut natural hair and a chiseled jaw Turner wanted to rock climb on.

Just like the image he'd been sent over the agency's emergency frequencies. He pulled it up on his brain-embedded computer (BECom for short) to double-check, the image floating in his field of view all thanks to a feed directly into his optic nerve. Perfect visual match. Now for the traditional test.

"We're closed, you know," Turner said, starting the script. If the man responded correctly, this was his guy. If not, well, hopefully he could just shoo him out into the street. The other options were... messy.

The man looked at him for a second and grunted. "I know, but I heard from my cousin you were the best cup of coffee near the port and I had to get some."

So far, so good. "That's true," Turner said. "Do you know what the secret ingredient is?"

"Nutmeg, and a dash of cardamom."

Turner made a face. "Does that sound gross to you? That sounds gross to me."

The big man chuckled. "Yeah, it kind of does. Confirm codename for me, please."

Turner blushed. He hated his codename. "Apple Turnover. Confirm your codename please."

"Pumpkin Spice," the big man said. It matched the dossier Turner had pulled up, and they both visibly relaxed. "I was told this place can act as an agency safehouse? I need to wait out the night. A ship's coming into dock in the morning to get me off the planet."

"You heard right. We've got a cot and supplies in the back room. Of course, I'll stick around tonight to watch your back. What'd you do to need to ditch off so quickly?" Turner said.

"Got caught in the depths of a high-security government facility putting taps on their datalinks."

Turner smiled. "Yeah, that'll do it. Good job getting out. You being pursued?

Spice looked nervous. "Uh, maybe. Almost definitely."

Turner's smile didn't waver. "Don't worry about it. We'll deal with it when they come. It's probably just local uniforms anyway. I've dealt with them before. But right now you're cold and wet. Would you like me to make you something while we wait for the fun to begin?"

The big guy smiled and Turner couldn't believe how cute it was, the way the smile crinkled his eyes. "Yeah, sure."

"Any preferences? Mocha, latte, just some drip?"

"How about you surprise me?"

"I think I've got just the thing," Turner said. "Oh, and let's network together and get sync permissions now in case we have trouble keeping your cover straight." They locked eyes for a split second, both BEComs dropping into discovery mode. Their BEComs synced, the initial connection making Turner feel like he was falling deep into Spice's eyes. Then Turner felt the tiny tug of an established connection, like a just-forgotten word on the tip of your tongue, before it settled into a familiar pathway out of the mind and he was back on stable ground again. Using it to send any sort of data was just like speaking a word or moving a certain way, requiring intentional, but near-reflexive, action. Right now the permissions were just mental audio and text to communicate on the sly, really low-bandwidth and nothing anyone looking at them could get a handle on as long as they kept straight faces while using it. Always useful for keeping a group's story straight.

Sync done, Turner turned and was surprised to realize he was sashaying as he went around behind the counter. A side effect of the excitement of getting to help a cutie evade the law, he supposed. He caught a glimpse in the reflection of the pastry case of Spice taking an appreciative look at his skinny ass. Huh, so things went both ways, did they?

Luckily he hadn't finished shutting down the machines yet. He ground some fresh espresso, tamped it, and let it start brewing.

"How do you feel about some extra flavor?" he asked as he started steaming the milk.

Spice leaned his hip against the counter. God, he made Turner feel short. Spice must have been at least a head taller. "Do you mean a flavor syrup? Vanilla, stuff like that?"

"Oh, far better than that." Turner went over and patted the top of his syrup dispenser. "This thing mixes nanomachines into the flavoring."

"For what, clean teeth?"

Turner waved a hand, dismissing the answer. "No, no. They carry memories, flashes of thought. Uses the BECom to let you experience them. Nothing overpowering by default, just a hint of each one. So, what do you say?"

Spice gave him a curious look. "Got anything in there that might help me calm down before the cops show up?"

"Are you kidding? I make that one for someone every day," Turner said.

He moved quickly after that. Foamed the milk and got the espresso into the cup, one of the special non-chipped mugs he kept around only for his favorite customers. Then he jacked into the machine using a direct neural link. Its interface was more intuitive this way. He pulled up some of his own memories and the machine synthesized the closest match from its database. After all, you didn't want customers getting to know you *that* well.

In went the special syrup, and the nicely foamed milk. He picked up a stirrer and started drawing in the foam. He paused for a second, stirrer stick in. He wanted to draw something fancy. Or cute. Show off a bit. But he couldn't think of anything. He'd never had this problem before. Then again, he'd just met this guy, and latte art was a very careful thing, especially when one was attracted to the drinker.

He thought about drawing a dong, because fuck subtlety, but he settled on drawing a pumpkin and an apple. Simplistic, but they worked. And he managed to render the individual ridges on the pumpkin, which he was pretty proud of.

Turner slid the cup across the counter to Pumpkin Spice before leaning on the waist-height (to him, at least) counter himself, his face just a little closer to the other man's. "So, excited to get back off this rock?" He caught Spice glancing around. "It's okay, I sweep the place for bugs every evening. And I've got top-level agency field clearance, so just take a drink and relax. We're clear, you can tell me anything."

"Yeah. It's just been a while since I had agency contact with anyone besides my handler. Give me a minute."

Turner held up his hands in a surrendering gesture and gave what he hoped was a reassuring nod. People who needed a safehouse were often skittish. Sometimes opening up right away helped them relax, sometimes they needed a bit of time.

Spice looked down at the cup and smiled. "Nice art. It's cute."

"Thanks."

Spice blew on the foam and took a long drink. His eyes widened in surprise. "Wow. I got... the smell after the first rain of the season, walking out on the once-dead earth as the new grass springs to life. Relaxing by the fire pit late at night, once the others have gone to sleep." He snorted and smiled. "And bubble baths."

"I thought you might like that last one. Feeling better?"

"Yes, thank you."

"Just keep drinking it and you'll be right as rain before the cops come along. We probably have another couple minutes, they're slow around here."

Spice took another long sip, and kept looking down into his cup as he spoke. "To answer your question, I'm definitely excited to get back. I've been out here for three months, and this planet isn't very much fun when you're spending most of your time crawling through maintenance ducts and planting bugs."

"Truly glamorous work. I'm surprised you aren't deep cover. People don't get sent out here for much else these days."

He shook his head. "I'm a terrible liar. That's why I got caught back there. They tried to train me, but it just never took." He looked at Turner and gave him a small smile.

Turner smiled right back. The big guy did have an honest face. "Anyone special back home you're looking forward to getting back to?" He normally didn't pry, but there was something about this one that made him want to know more.

Spice looked down into the mug again and took another sip before continuing. "Not really. You know, our job makes you travel a lot when you're field. Everyone I know thinks I work for an interplanetary shipping company. It sucks I can't tell them what's really going on. Then again, I'm gone so often it'd be hard to set down roots with anyone, even if I could tell them the truth."

Turner nodded. He knew how that felt. "Everyone I know thinks I own a coffee shop. Which I do, on paper. But I've got some great stories about this place being used as a safehouse, and no one to share them with. Plus it's always awkward when they ask what I did before all this," he said, waving a hand to indicate the shop. (He'd done wet-work and specialized in brain-hacking. When people asked about his past he told them he'd worked in marketing, which he figured was worse.) "So believe me, I understand." He reached across the counter and patted the big man's hand, letting his fingertips linger for a long moment, before brushing them across Spice's knuckles as he retreated. "It can be hard to get that human connection."

Spice looked down at his hand, and over at Turner. "Yeah, yeah it can. Do they train you safehouse guys as therapists?"

"No. I just run a coffee shop with a really chatty clientele. And I like forming these kinds of connections."

"Even if they're temporary?"

"Those can be the best kinds. It's amazing how honest you can be when you only have a few hours together at most."

"Is that so," Spice said. It came out flat, and his eyes were far away.

Turner turned back to the machines and started making himself a drink just to busy his hands, stop himself from worrying he'd stepped on a conversational land mine. "Yeah. You should try it sometime. If you get a chance."

"I'm really more of a long-term guy."

"Nothing wrong with that." Turner felt stupid for bringing this up. He didn't have a lot of game, and he knew it. It all seemed to just be making Spice feel worse, which is definitely not what he wanted. He looked down and found he'd made himself a mocha on autopilot. Okay, then. Apparently his subconscious thought it was comfort time for him, and that chocolate was better than any memory.

He quickly changed the subject, sharing old stories of ops gone hilariously wrong. It turned out Spice had a similar cache of tales, and they spent the next half hour in a competition for who had experienced the more disastrously fucked operation.

There was loud banging on the door, and they both started, looking up to see a very grumpy looking police officer glaring in at them.

Turner winked at Spice. "Even slower than usual. Just play it cool and let me do the talking."

Spice nodded and gulped down the rest of his drink. Turner casually walked out from behind the counter, giving his hips a little extra roll as he went because he was determined to show off. Plus, it helped him walk slower as he double-checked his and Spice's BECom sync. All green.

He unlocked the door and let the officer in. "Why Officer Legras, we're closed. But feel free to come on in and dry off."

The officer stamped her boots on the sidewalk, shaking off the worst of the rain, and stepped inside. She gave Turner a level look, her strong face fixed in a humorless expression that was only diluted a little by the explosion of golden curls sticking out from under her hat. "I'm here as part of an investigation. Your customer here," she nodded at Spice, "matches the description of a man we're searching for on suspicion of breaking and entering into a government facility. I'm able to take him on that suspicion alone, to be part of a line-up." She turned to Spice. "Sir, if you'd come with me please."

Turner interposed himself between the officer and Spice. "Officer, officer, don't be so hasty. This gentleman has been in my shop since I started closing up over an hour and a half ago."

What are you doing? Spice asked over their sync up.

Just follow along, Turner sent back.

Legras grunted. "Do you have proof of that?" This was an old dance she and Turner had done a half-dozen times by now. He wondered sometimes if she had ever figured out it was more than just coincidence that kept bringing her back here.

"Of course," he said with a smile. "Let me just pull out the video from the security feed." He pulled up the video on his BECom and ran a special program. It took all the angles of Spice since he walked into the shop and composited them into a digital version of the man, then inserted him into the scene, starting about half an hour before closing. The agency paid for the fastest BEComs, and by the time Officer Legras handed him her tablet to transfer the file over, everything was already done. Turner killed his connection with Spice before syncing with the tablet, just in case they had a sniffer installed on it to log connected networks. With a quick command he then synched to the tablet and transferred the files over. The huge video files made the process take whole seconds, a virtual eternity. "And there you go," he said with his most trustworthy grin as he disconnected from the tablet.

Legras looked down at her tablet, jumping back and forth through the file, which contained the standard previous eight hours of footage. "Well, looks like this holds up," she said, stowing the tablet in its pocket on her thigh. "But you and I both know this isn't enough. I'm going to have to get this looked over to see if it's doctored, and I can't just let him walk away while we run it through our systems." She turned back to Spice. "Sir, I'm going to have to ask you some questions, just to be sure there's enough reasonable doubt to not take you in."

Spice blanched. "Um, sure. I mean, of course." He glanced at Turner and was already looking panicked. But despite his panic he was smart, and had his BECom set up to reconnect. Turner met his eyes and re-established the sync.

Play it as cool as you can, Turner sent over the sync. *I'm here to back you up.* He turned back to Legras. "Officer, would you like some coffee? I haven't quite finished shutting everything down. Been distracted." He glanced over meaningfully at Spice.

When she looked at him her eyes softened. "Sure. Thanks, Turner."

"Anytime," he said. He went back behind the counter quickly and let himself make coffee on automatic as he started running through files and scripts, doctoring documents as fast as he could. Every template and macro he'd set up might not be enough for pulling a trick this fast.

"Sir, what's your name?" Legras asked.

Your name is Oliver Jackson, he sent Spice over the link.

"Jackson. Uh, Oliver Jackson."

"Do you live around here? Or are you visiting?"

Turner fed data into all the fields on a fake ID in the span of a blink. He wasn't even paying attention to pouring the coffee anymore, just staring at the windows floating in front of his eyes, hoping Legras didn't notice him tense up. Okay, ID done. Travel records—

"Sir?"

Tell her you're visiting.

"Visiting, sorry," Spice said. Turner wasn't even looking at him but could tell from his voice he was uncomfortable. Possibly enough to blow his cover. Crap.

"I'll need your travel records and ID. Receipts too, if you have them." Turner threw a large handful in there. He flinched as he saw a restaurant receipt timestamped at 4 A.M. slip in, but too late to fix that now. "If they all check out, we should be done for tonight, at least."

He heard Spice choke.

No, no, you're fine. Here. He queued up the transfer, a big bundle of files, and Spice accepted. The documents started downloading, but it was taking longer than Turner had hoped.

Stall her just a moment. Ask her something. Anything.

"Y—yes officer. Does your tablet connect with BEComs?"

"Definitely," she said, pulling out and handing over the tablet.

The files finished transferring just as Spice killed his connection to prevent the tablet from possibly sniffing out their link.

Turner let out a quiet sigh of relief and finished pouring the coffee into a to-go cup. He brought it over as Spice transferred the data.

"Here's your coffee, officer," Turner said, handing over the cup. She took a sip as she looked over the data on the tablet Spice handed back to her.

"Well," she said, after a long minute, "this all seems to check out. Oh, wait." Turner saw the 4 A.M. receipt pulled up on the screen. "Weird, I didn't think this place was open that late."

Silence hung in the air like a hawk ready to strike.

"Oh," she chuckled, "right. I forgot they just started doing 24-hour takeout."

Turner barely choked down the sigh of relief that tried to escape his throat.

"Everything looks good for now," she said with a nod to Spice. She turned to Turner. "I've got one last question for you, though: why is he still here, if you've been closing up?"

Turner winked at her. "Oh, I let the cute ones stay longer." He glanced at Spice and saw the big man blushing. He knew he could make that honest face work in his favor. "After all, I'd rather have something nice to look at while I clean up."

The officer chuckled. "You never change, Turner. I'll still need to have this video looked over, you got that?"

"I would expect nothing less from the finest officer of the law."

Legras rolled her eyes at that, but there was a smile on her lips as she turned to walk out the door. Turner held it open for her.

"Good luck with your search, Officer. And I'll see you in the morning for your mocha."

Legras waved over her shoulder as she walked back off into the night. Turner quickly locked the door behind her and turned to Spice with a grin.

"I can't believe you pulled that off," Spice said, visibly sagging in relief. Turner patted him on the shoulder as he went back to the counter.

"Of course I did. It all went like clockwork," Turner said, but for once in his life he let his face show how close it had been, how lucky they'd gotten. Spice chuckled, and the big man's posture relaxed further.

It felt weird for Turner to be so open with someone. Good, even. He wished he had someone to do it with all the time. He'd hardly taken a moment to breathe when his mouth, working too far ahead of his brain, let something spill out. "So you're really only a long-term guy, huh?"

Spice looked embarrassed. "Yeah. I mean, don't get me wrong, I'm flattered. I just—don't do that well in the short term, sometimes. I get attached."

"Nothing wrong with that," Turner said, trying not to squirm as he realized he repeated himself from earlier, more to convince himself than to assure Spice. He poured himself some water, took a long drink, and spent a good amount of time looking at the counter. The awkward silence descended like fog rolling in off the ocean.

But when he looked at Spice he saw Spice looking at him. "Hey," Spice said. Silence hung between them for a long moment. "Don't get me wrong, we can still enjoy each other's company. You're pretty good to talk to. I don't get a lot of people I feel like I can open up to, but I feel really comfortable around you. Any chance I could get some contact info?"

"Uh, sure." Turner wasn't going to look a consolation prize in the mouth. A few commands and his info beamed over to Spice. "That's all a secure line, so you can say whatever you want."

"How heavily do the bosses monitor it?"

Turner shrugged. "It's a personal line, so enough to know if we're betraying them, but that's about it. They don't care about fraternization between agents anyway, no matter what form that takes. We're progressive that way. Whatever you need to talk about, just shoot me a message. Text, audio, video, hologram if we set it up ahead of time. I'm easy to get a hold of."

"Thanks," Spice said. He gave Turner a queer look. "Uh, hey, is there any chance you have some spare clothes? I've had worse nights than sitting around in damp clothing, but given the opportunity I'd really like to be dry."

Turner smacked himself in the forehead. "Yeah, yeah, of course. Sorry, the whole police thing knocked me off my host game." He got up from the counter, and the two headed for the back of the shop.

He opened the supply closet, then the panel marked "utility access" in the back of it. A quick flick of a hidden switch and the wall swung open to reveal a small room, no bigger than twelve feet by twelve feet, stuffed to the brim with equipment and supplies. A small cot with a thin mattress, blanket, and a single pillow sat in the corner. There was a shallow gun cage on the wall (locked, of course) below which was crammed a tiny desk and terminal. Various other sundries were stuffed on wire shelves running along two walls.

Turner looked Spice up and down, then turned and grabbed a towel, a pair of jeans and boxers, and a black t-shirt off a shelf. He tossed him the towel first, and set the clothes down on the bed. "That should be enough to get you dry, and the clothing should fit. You're bigger than my usual, so it might be a little tight. Sorry there's no shower. We do have some of that dry shower crap they give you for backcountry assignments."

"This is good, thanks." Spice walked past him and started toweling off.

Turner leaned against the door, facing out towards the shop. He tried really, really hard not to turn around, not to look at something he knew he couldn't have, but kept sneaking glances over his shoulder. Spice had pulled off his shirt, revealing a body heavy with muscle with just a little padding over the top, making him look functional instead of like some steroids-and-starvation model. Turner's better sense gave up and he stared. But subtly. He had some dignity to maintain after all.

Spice caught his eye just as he was about to pull off his wet pants. "Getting an eyeful, Turnover?"

Turner cleared his throat and looked away. "Sorry, sorry."

He could hear the blush in Spice's voice. "It's okay. Kind of flattering, actually. But, you know, long term."

Turner swallowed. "We could message, if you wanted." He heard Spice zipping up his fly and the rustle of the new shirt being pulled over his head. "Just a thought. It... wouldn't have to be a one-night thing. Just long distance. That is, if you're interested and not just trying to let me down gently." He knew a lot about that.

He heard Spice stop moving. "No. No, it's not that at all." Suddenly he felt the bulk of the man close behind him, warmth radiating between them. "It's just been a long time for me, since I've been with someone. I get real nervous. And I have to admit, this wasn't really what I was expecting to happen tonight. Safehouse experiences are usually far more boring. Or abjectly terrifying."

Turner laughed. "Yeah, yeah."

Then there were strong hands on his shoulders. "Would you really call?"

Turner wanted to melt into that grip. Those warm hands were turning his knees to jelly. "Yes. Yes I would. Every damn day if you want me to."

Spice gently turned Turner around, keeping his strong hands on Turner's shoulders. "Then why don't we see where things go?"

Turner looked up into those deep brown eyes, flecks of gold giving them a sparkle. Then they were getting closer. And closer.

He leaned into the kiss, Spice's hands sliding down as the big man wrapped his arms around him, one on his shoulder blade, the other on this lower back. It was a strong kiss, firm, and he had to brace himself against it, stepping back against the door frame with his hands on Spice's chest. He arched his back, pressing his front into Spice's. They held there for a long moment, Turner's hands on Spice's absolute granite slabs of pecs. Slowly they separated, and he felt Spice's warm breath on his chin and neck.

"You're pretty good," Turner said breathily.

"Not so bad yourself," Spice said, and there was that shy smile that had probably disqualified him from undercover training but damn if it wasn't cute.

Turner slowly slid from Spice's grip out into the supply closet until just their hands touched, then he grasped Spice's hands, drawing him back out into the front of the shop. A quick hip-check of a small button on the wall made all the windows one-way. They could see the storm but no one out there could see them.

"Going to butter me up with another drink?"

"If you like. But mostly that cot is far too cramped for my tastes."

Without a word Spice leaned down, wrapping a big arm around Turner's thighs, another around his waist, and hefting him up onto the serving counter. Turner went with it, then wrapped his legs around Spice's waist, drawing him in, grinding himself against those strong abdominals. He wrapped his arms around Spice's neck and trailed kisses along Spice's jaw, down his neck, down to the cleft between his clavicles.

Spice let out a soft moan and leaned in, leaving a lingering kiss on Turner's neck, then sucking at it, just a bit, warm and hot. Turner's hardness stretched his jeans taut. Spice rumbled with satisfaction and ground his hips forward, rubbing Turner just the right way. Turner slid his hands down to Spice's muscular buttocks and drew him in harder, grinding together as Spice slowly moved down his neck, nibbling at his clavicle.

Spice's strong hands slipped under Turner's shirt, along lean flanks and bony hips. The man's strong fingers hooked under the edge of the shirt and Turner lifted up his arms, letting Spice pull it off over him. Spice laid him back on the counter, cold quartz raising goosebumps on his back as Spice trailed lingering kisses down his front, along his sternum and down past his navel. He arched in pleasure as Spice got to just above where his fly was buttoned.

Spice looked up at him, resting his chin on Turner's stomach. "Do you want this?"

Turner marshaled his thoughts back into some sort of coherency, which was as difficult as telling a hurricane to go to its room. "Yes. You do, right?"

Spice smiled. "Absolutely." He left another kiss on Turner's stomach and ran his hands up and down Turner's thighs. Turner took the opportunity, hooking his feet under the hem of Spice's shirt and, with a flex of his abs, raised his hips as he straightened his legs, tugging the shirt off over Spice's head as soon as the man lifted up his arms.

"I figured it was only fair," Turner said.

"Nice trick."

Turner wrapped his legs around Spice's now-bare waist. "I'm full of them." He opened up their sync channel further, requesting full sensory access.

"What's that?" Spice said, pausing with a confused look on his face.

"I modified the syrup machine's program a while back so I can share sensations, current or saved, from one user's memory to another's. They can be real-time, too, with no annoying permission pauses, if you give me full access. The wonders of pure sensation transmission." He sat up and kissed Spice on the neck again, right below the curve of his jaw. "What do you say?"

"Sounds interesting. I'm in." And just like that the permissions were unlocked and they synced up completely, full-access. Nothing was transmitting right now, but there was a baseline awareness, beneath conscious thought, of the other man's body's feelings.

Where his hands were, his excitement, trepidation buried by lust and curiosity. Turner smiled, trying to cover up his own nervousness, and started curating sensations from his databanks. Spice looked at him expectantly.

"Hey, I didn't tell you to stop what you were doing." Turner said with a smile.

"Good," Spice said. He undid Turner's pants button and slowly unzipped the fly.

Then those strong hands were on Turner's hips, stripping his pants off, slowly, inch by inch, fingers stroking newly exposed skin as they slid down Turner's legs. Spice finished yanking them off and then went back to paying attention to Turner's stomach. Turner moaned as his naked cock rubbed against Spice's front.

"Don't get too excited now," Spice said. "The main show hasn't even started yet." He gave a long lick to one of Turner's nipples, and Turner felt a little shock run through him. Then Spice made his way back down Turner's body, and soon he was nibbling at the man's thighs, tantalizingly close to Turner's throbbing erection, but not quite touching it. Turner sent the first sensation back through the BECom, a quick copy of the feel of Spice's lips on the sensitive skin of his inner thigh, and he felt Spice tense up in surprise, then let out a soft sound of enjoyment.

"Now that is a nice trick," Spice said, as Turner kept sending the sensations through live, on a slight delay. Soon he overlaid them for Spice, creating the sensation of many mouths on the skin, all of them tender and persistent, warmth blooming in a dozen wonderful spots. He gave himself a dose too, ghost kisses running up and down his thighs, and felt himself grow harder.

Turner sat up then and leaned over, putting his mouth next to Spice's ear. He gave it a nibble, and felt a gratifying shiver run through Spice.

"Look in the little wood box under the counter."

Spice looked up at him on confusion and then bent over further, digging through the junk on the shelf. In a few seconds there was a slight crinkle of foil.

"Pumpkin spice?" Spice said, laughter in his voice.

"It is my favorite flavor. You should try it," Turner said, gently running his hands under Spice's jaw as the big man looked up at him.

"I think I will," Spice said. He opened the condom, and slowly, fingers teasing at every step, unrolled it over Turner's hard-on.

Turner ran his hands along Spice's cheeks and wrapped his fingers in the other man's hair, taking him in for another long, hard kiss. Then the big man went down on him, running his tongue up Turner's shaft before putting his mouth over the head and starting to suck. Turner pressed his bare thighs against Spice's delightful stubble, just enough texture to excite him, and pulled Spice even closer, tangling his finger's in the other man's hair.

Spice did amazing things as he sucked, with tongue and lips, changing tactics as soon as Turner got used to one or the other. Spice's hands ran up along Turner's thighs and gripped at his ass, using it as leverage as he played Turner like a two-dollar fiddle. Turner fed all the sensations back through the BECom link to Spice, along with the wet warmth of being submerged in a hot tub, and the tingle of hands running up and down one's back, tracing along the spine. Spice groaned, making Turner smile, and then worked harder, enjoying the results of his own work on Turner's cock.

Turner arched his back in pleasure at Spice's vigor, and soon he couldn't hold it in any longer. He let out a shuddering gasp as he came explosively. Spice kept sucking till the end, making Turner come far longer than usual, his mind near blank, all coherent thought overridden with the bursts of pleasure.

He let himself flop back on the cold counter with a delighted moan, and Spice came up with him, Turner's legs hooked over his shoulders, his head between Turner's thighs. Slowly the big man disentangled himself, gently stroking his hands on Turner's calves and locking gazes as they did so. Spice took the condom off, knotted it, and threw it in the trash bin as he and Turner held each other's gaze.

Turner sat up slowly and smiled. "Don't worry, I'm not going to leave you out in the cold."

"You hardly have," Spice said, but Turner knew through their link, that background awareness, that his partner hadn't orgasmed yet, and he intended to fix that.

He stood up and then pressed Spice back against the espresso machine, tracing the bigger man's muscles with delicate fingertips. He sucked Spice's neck, and rubbed his hand over the telltale bulge in Spice's jeans. With a smile he undid the button.

"Now then," Turner said, "you get to go a step further." He ran his hands down inside the back of Spice's pants and gave his muscular ass a squeeze before bringing them around to the front, massaging the other man's balls and rubbing his shaft. He felt a warm wetness on his palm as Spice's pre-cum dribbled down. Then he drew his hands out of the man's pants and gave Spice a wicked smile while gazing right into his gorgeous eyes. Spice's breath hitched.

Turner smiled before undoing Spice's pants and drawing them down to the floor. And while was down there he recovered two very important items from under the counter.

"Now how about we get that steam wand of yours ready to go?" he said, sharing a long kiss with Spice as he opened the condom. He unrolled it onto Spice quickly, with practiced hands.

"Of course, first we have to wipe it down," he said. He rubbed the lube from the little bottle in his other hand up and down Spice's shaft. Spice grunted in animalistic pleasure. "And I want to be sure you're okay with this," he said as he pressed himself up against Spice, their stomachs and chests pressed together, Spice's hardness against his belly, his lips against the other man's neck.

"Absolutely," Spice said, and it came out as a purr of pleasure with a growl backing it. Turner hopped back up on the counter, leading Spice closer to him by the hand, and then leaned back and spread his legs wide.

Spice wasted no time taking advantage of such an invitation. He leaned in for a long kiss, one hand on each of Turner's thighs. As he kept the kiss going, he picked up the lube and covered his fingers with it, and dipped one into Turner's anus, taking no time before finding Turner's prostate and giving it a good massage, sending shivers of excitement through Turner's body. Then soon two fingers, then three.

"You ready?" Spice said, drawing back a bit. Turner felt loosened up and ready for anything.

Turner smiled. "I am so ready. Come on, jack into me like you do into an insecure datalink network."

He felt the vibration of Spice's chuckle where the big man's sides pressed against his thighs. "I'll try not to set off any alarms." Spice glanced outside. "You know, given the season, I've always wanted to do this in the rain."

Turner smiled and sent though the appropriate commands, pulling sensations from the database and sending them down the link. Soon they felt drops of water cascading over them, the sensations as real to their minds as anything: a moderate rain that was just the right temperature, cool but not cold. Turner felt goosebumps rise up on his thighs as Spice smiled at him. He'd rendered it so it took into account where they covered each other, raindrops pattering onto and running down his face, shoulders and legs, but dry where Spice stood over him.

Spice leaned down and kissed him hard, then slipped inside him, warm and slick. The man's girth was impressive, just on the inside of manageable, and Turner gripped the counter hard as he stretched to accommodate. Spice leaned over him, thrusting slowly, twisting just a bit this way and that, stimulating all his nerves till every one tingled with pleasure.

He wrapped his legs around Spice, urging the other man to go deeper with each thrust, reveling in the warmth and cold and universal wet taking his body to opposing extremes. Spice obliged, and arched over further, locking lips with Turner as he plowed harder and deeper. Turner made his lips taste like an apple turnover still warm from the oven, and Spice dove in a little more hungrily, licking at Turner's lips and mingling their tongues together even as he smiled at the joke.

Turner flexed his abs to sit up just a bit, wrapping his legs around Spice's strong body for support, and curled over to suck at the man's neck between his own gasps of pleasure, using the BECom to add a bit of extra flavor to the man's already delightful skin. He'd never felt so comfortable with someone inside him, and adding the taste of pumpkin spice to the experience made it more heavenly then he could imagine.

Spice reached down between them and grabbed Turner's erect-again cock, playing his fingers over the head and jerking slowly along the shaft, slick with the lube still on his hand. Turner lost himself in the carnal pleasure of the moment, all heat and lust and the thrill of nerves riding on the edge of climax, a cliff that only got better, more tempting to plunge off of, the longer they rode along it.

"I'm coming," Spice gasped in his ear, his breath hot and wet, and Turner felt the telltale jerk inside of him as Spice shot his load. One particular jerk and thrust combined to light Turner's pleasure centers like a Christmas tree, and Turner let out an explosive breath as he came, spattering cum all over his and Spice's chest.

Spice leaned down on top of him as he lay back on the counter, and they both stayed there pressed together for a long minute, their heat merging, sweaty bodies and breath all in unison.

After that they slowly drew apart. Spice disposed of the condom, but when Turner reached for some napkins to clean up the mess he'd created, Spice gently grabbed his wrist. The bigger man reached over and grabbed a clean rag from under the counter, ran it under the steamer for a quick second, and proceeded to gently wipe up the mess, stretching out each rub against Turner's skin.

"Hey, give me access to the database," Spice said.

Turner was enjoying himself, so why not? He granted Spice access, and a few moments later the sensation of warm wet cotton changed to that of dry silk, sliding smooth over his chest.

Turner felt himself breaking into a grin. Once Spice was done he kneeled down and cleaned Spice off the same way, playing on sensations of warm silk and textured rag, lingering longer than was strictly necessary, enjoying listening to Spice's relaxed breathing and its slight changes as he cleaned.

He stood, tossing the rag in the bin, and they each wrapped an arm around each other before making their way slowly back to the saferoom on bare feet. Turner only half-remembered to shut the doors behind them before they collapsed in a mutually sweaty heap on the bed.

They cuddled together on the narrow cot, faces inches away from each other, all tired grins and smiles.

"I always knew Pumpkin Spice was my favorite flavor," Turner said, leaning in and brushing his lips against Spice's, the briefest of kisses.

"I'm glad I'm here, at least for a while, with you," Spice said. He brought Turner a little closer, and Turner rested his head on the man's chest.

"Think you can come back?"

Despite Legras's insinuations to the contrary, Turner never had much luck with the local boys. Had to keep them locked out of a huge portion of his life. But here was someone he could share everything with, no reservations, no secrets. That was worth holding onto.

Spice leaned down and kissed him. Spice's lips tasted better than anything Turner could manufacture. "I can guarantee I can be back at least once a year, no matter where they send me." Spice paused. "So I take it you really want this to be more than just a temporary connection?"

"Yes. Turns out sometimes they're not the best kind. And it's... it's nice to be able to share the whole truth."

Spice smiled. "Okay then. How do you feel about a holo call in three ISO days? Once I'm clear of this planet, have a chance to get situated again?"

"Only if I can message you before then."

Spice's smile broke out into an unrestrained grin. "Absolutely."

"And I'll see what I can do about getting that sensation-sharing tech to work over the holo connection."

"I'd like that."

Turner had never jumped into a relationship like this, and certainly not a quasi-long-distance relationship with someone he'd just met. But it felt right, and even if it was a mistake, he had to give it a go. Some mistakes were worth making. "I'm glad," he said.

He cuddled a little further into Spice's arms, and the two fell asleep together on the narrow cot, intertwined, the only noise besides their peaceful breathing the pounding of the rain outside.

The Closing Shift
JJ Poulos

Ramona loved the closing shift.

The quiet swish of the broom, collecting crumbly bits of muffins. The scent of cleaner and the gleam of a dozen wet matte tables. Hot clouds of steam from the sanitizer and the glint of the clean espresso machine. She loved smelling like cleaner and coffee and hard work. She loved turning off the lights on a sparkling, organized coffee bar, locking the doors, and walking home in the dark.

Ramona loved the bleary college students who came in for their last minute red-eyes. She loved the self-important suits who never tipped and asked for their non-fat no-foam sugar-free vanilla lattes, the most soulless drink in the entire universe. She loved the older patrons and their foamy, decaf lattes, never finished but always savored. The closing shift was quiet and organized and everything Ramona needed.

And then something threw a wrench into Ramona's job, Ramona's universe, Ramona's very fiber.

Anne, Ramona's boss, dropped the bag of beans without ceremony on her pristine, still-damp floor.

"How are you?" She gave Ramona a warm, friendly hug. She smelled like herbal shampoo and pencil shavings, her body strong and humming with energy. Ramona had wanted to sleep with her boss since she'd started working at the coffee shop. She was bisexual and had that adorable, middle-aged athletic lesbian thing going on. She gave a lot of hugs, and Ramona always wanted them to last longer.

"We got a new variety of espresso bean! Do you have plans tonight?"

"Just going home and studying," Ramona said.

"Mind staying late?"

Visions of Anne on the desk in the back room danced through Ramona's head. "Not at all."

"Great! You'll need to empty the hopper, scrub it, and then put the new beans in. They're fantastic, a whole new kind of super rare bean. I'll be in early tomorrow to get the grind tested." She hugged her again. "You're the best. See you later!"

And then she was gone, and the smile dropped off Ramona's face.

She locked the doors and turned up her Pandora station and started in on the espresso hopper, trying to work out the hum in her body, the wet warmth that persisted between her legs, the insistent picture in her mind of Anne on the desk in back, leaning on the coffee bag, papers under her, and Ramona's face buried—

She scrubbed and scrubbed, willing the image out of her mind.

Finally the hopper was sparkling, and she turned to the new bag of beans. It was made of rough burlap, covered in writing she couldn't even begin to read, and beautiful, colorful swirling lines.

She grabbed a scissors and sliced the bag open.

The scent that burst out was unlike anything she'd smelled. It was dark and rich and flowery. The beans were glossy with oil and slid about as if they were alive. Ramona closed her eyes and breathed in the smell. She opened her eyes and, leaving the bag on the ground, turned to grab the hopper.

There was a water-like patter as the bag tipped over, as the beans danced across the floor.

"Shit," Ramona said, before turning around.

Far too large for the bag, like a coffee bean that sprouted into a tree and then grew until it burst from the bag's darkness, and then grew some more, a woman lay. She was dark like the espresso beans and she gleamed glossily, like they did. They spilled around her like rose petals.

"Thank you for letting me out," she said, smiling a brilliant smile.

Ramona made a strangled noise. "Where did you come from?"

"Originally? Or just now?"

Ramona's mouth opened and closed, wordlessly.

"I was in there," she pointed to the bag at her feet. "I was sleeping on my tree when the beans were picked, I think. I only woke up a little while ago." She stood up and stretched, her body endlessly elongating. She seemed to be as tall as a tree for a moment.

"How—that's not possible. You're way too large to fit in that bag." The woman smiled. "My size changes. I was sleeping in a coffee cherry. I'm—mmm. You could call me a dryad, I suppose."

"That's not possible."

The dryad laughed. "You seem to think a lot of things aren't possible. Here." She stepped up to the counter, laid her dark hand against the blue marble, and trailed her fingers across it, slow and sensual. Where her hand had been, leaves—dark and ridged—and little white flowers sprung up, as if they had been growing there all along. Ramona gave a little cry and reached out to touch the cool dark leaves, the delicate white flowers.

"You're a dryad."

She laughed. "I am. And you saved me. Now I can go back to my tree."

"We're pretty far away from places that grow coffee trees," Ramona said, feeling suddenly guilty. "Do you—you might—we should find you a plane ticket or something."

The dryad laughed again. "That's very kind of you, but now that I am free, I will make it just fine." She walked around the counters, her head tilted, her fingers touching everything, but leaving no leaves. "So this is where my beans go."

"Y-yes, though we've not had this kind of bean before. Your kind of bean."

The dryad nodded. "Do people like their coffee here? Do they respect it?"

Ramona felt herself nodding with perhaps too much vigor. "We take great care to make the highest quality drinks. People are always coming back—they love it."

"Good."

She turned back towards Ramona. "Before I go—you helped

me with my problem. I would like to help you with your problem."

Ramona felt her face heat up. "I—I don't have any problems—"

The dryad stepped towards Ramona, a small, confident smile on her lips. "I am a coffee dryad. Coffee brings warmth to the body—it makes hearts race. It readies bodies." She stepped towards her again. "Your body—your heart—is already warmed. I heard—I felt—you talking to that woman."

"My boss," Ramona murmured. The dryad nodded. She stepped closer—Ramona was surrounded by the scent of coffee beans. Up close the dryad was now, somehow, the same height as Ramona. She was suddenly acutely aware that the creature wore no clothes—that her breasts were small and pert, that her hips curved just a little, that she looked soft and very, very close. The dryad ran a finger down Ramona's dark hair, braided over her shoulder. She had no hair of her own, her head round and dark.

"Your boss. You were very disappointed by her. May I—warm you?"

Ramona took a deep, shaky breath. "Yes," she whispered.

The dryad reached one long arm around Ramona and pulled her close, kissing her. Her lips tasted like dark, rich coffee, deep and complex. They parted for a moment, and Ramona took another deep breath, delirious with the dryad's rich scent and delicious lips.

She caught her gaze, brown eyes reflecting brown eyes. Ramona touched the dryad's long neck and they kissed again, urgently. The dryad's lips parted, and Ramona tasted something lighter, brighter, the warmth of her tongue intoxicating. She needed more of it. More.

Ramona wrapped her arms around the dryad's frame, her hands resting on the perfect, bare curve above her bottom. She pulled her close, kissing deeper, lost in the sweet taste of her kiss and the intense heat of their commingling bodies.

Still kissing, the dryad's hands found the buttons of Ramona's shirt, and began to unbutton it. She shivered with pleasure as the cool air kissed her skin, as the dryad's fingers brushed the round of her stomach, as they moved up her body. She pulled away as the last button came undone, and she stared at Ramona as she slipped the shirt gently off her shoulders.

"Mm—ah—what—what should I call you?" Ramona asked. "Do you have a name?"

The dryad thought for a moment.

"The last human I laid with called me Chaoua."

"Chaoua," Ramona said.

"I hope, though, that you won't be able to say much of anything for very much longer."

Ramona's knees went weak.

The dryad laid a path of sweet kisses across Ramona's shoulders as she tugged at her bra. Her breasts spilled out, and Chaoua took them in her narrow hands and caressed them lovingly. Her palms were slightly rough, like the bark of a young tree, and the sensation against Ramona's nipples made her whimper. The dryad was smiling a wicked smile.

"You are melting like oil in the hot sun. Do not melt too fast. I want to taste you."

Ramona moaned, unable to contain her excitement, all the more excited to hear her sexual sounds echo in the empty coffee house. Chaoua smiled and unzipped Ramona's pants, slipped her out of her boots and pants and then Ramona was naked, there, behind the counter. She turned and carefully folded the clothes and stacked them on the counter. Ramona watched her supple body moving, and suddenly needed to touch it, to know what every inch of her skin felt like. She stepped forward and began kissing the sweet, tender valleys and hills of her back, from her strong shoulders to the dimples of her bottom. She went back to the dryad's neck and, then her breasts. They were soft and warm and Chaoua made the most beautiful noises when Ramona touched them.

Ramona guided her like that to the counter top, between the bakery case and the cash register, and lifted her gently onto it.

"So cold!" The dryad squeaked.

"We'll warm it," Ramona said, parting her legs. It had been a long time since she had touched anyone besides herself, and it was thrilling. Chaoua was thrilling.

Chaoua leaned down to kiss her, to run her hands over Ramona's body. Chaoua was wet, and Ramona trailed her fingers through the moisture on her inner thighs before gently parting her inner lips.

"Yes, please," Chaoua whispered. Her brown eyes were shut, and her face was intent, concentrating. Her lower lip caught in her teeth as Ramona slid two fingers into Chaoua's slick vulva. Her thumb found her clitoris and she stroked it with gentle, reverent touches. Chaoua gasped and bucked against Ramona's hand. There was a smell of coffee in the air—not the deep, flowery aroma of the beans, but the smell of coffee brewing, a hot, wet, urgent smell.

"More," Chaoua said, and Ramona slid another finger in, and another. Chaoua bucked against Ramona's hand, urgent. Her skin carried the dark sheen of sweat, her nipples were hard, and her hands clutched at Ramona as if she were drowning. Her writhing was everything, but Ramona needed to know how she tasted.

She leaned her head over and ran her tongue over her clit. The dryad gave a cry of joy. She tasted sweeter than Ramona had expected—she'd expected perhaps something like a well-pulled espresso shot, but Chaoua lacked that bitterness. Still, she tasted of coffee, a smooth, slightly musky taste, rich and good. Ramona pushed her tongue against Chaoua's clitoris and licked with firm, long strokes, feeling Chaoua tighten around her fingers, feeling her body twitch, her clitoris pulse under the adoring lapping of her tongue.

Ramona stopped her tonguing long enough to kiss those delicate breasts again, to find the dryad's mouth and kiss it, too. Chaoua's mouth was dry from moaning and eager, desperate for attention. Ramona stared into her beautiful green eyes as she fucked her to orgasm, the dryad riding her hand with frantic, wanton need, screaming and arching in glorious, lusty beauty.

She curled over Ramona's body, her head resting on Ramona's shoulder, forehead pressed into the curls that had escaped her ponytail. Ramona continued to gleefully tease her, delicately pressing her clitoris as it pulsed, sliding her fingers in and out and around the wonderful wet mess that was the dryad's vulva.

"Stop," she whimpered, and Ramona slowly, remorsefully, removed her hand. She glanced down and gasped. Her fingers, her dripping palm, the floor, and the counter top soaked in coffee flowers. Tiny white drips of flowers, individually spotting the floor, and a cluster so big between her legs it was impossible to see the marble between the petals. Ramona opened her hand and the flowers gently floated from her palm to the ground, as if unconcerned by gravity's pull.

Chaoua gave a luxurious chuckle. "I made a mess." She hopped off the counter, leaving the puddle of brilliant white flowers perfect and unbothered.

She dropped to her knees in front of Ramona, her hairless, dark head coming up to her chest. Chaoua kissed her breasts again, taking one nipple into her mouth and one in her fingertips and teasing them gently, then harder and harder until Ramona thought she might come just then. Chaoua switched to the other, and sucked on it, teasing her sore, wet nipple with the tips of her fingers. Ramona held on to the coffee counter until her hands hurt.

Chaoua left a trail of kisses down her round stomach, and over her hips. Ramona giggled and squirmed. She left glossy coffee-oil spots where her lips lingered.

"Just a taste—" she said teasingly, her breath hot over the crease between Ramona's thigh and her mound. Ramona held her breath, the anticipation overwhelming and absolutely perfect. A moan, jagged and ecstatic and loud enough to fill the empty coffee house, bubbled out of her, as Chaoua brought her warm lips to Ramona's wet, swollen mound.

Her mouth was electric, shooting pleasure through Ramona's body. She felt herself riding Chaoua's mouth desperately, Chaoua's hands cupping her butt cheeks and squeezing them gently.

Ramona lay her hands over Chaoua's warm, bare head for something to tether herself to reality as she lost herself in intense waves of pleasure. Her orgasm shook her and lasted an eternity and left her weak and giddy.

Chaoua sat down, pulling Ramona down onto her lap. Ramona practically fell, her legs jelly and her breath ragged, laughing. Chaoua kissed her gently, her face messy.

Chaoua held her up with one strong arm, and slipped her other between Ramona's legs. Ramona was perhaps more wet and excited than she'd ever been, and Chaoua's fingers felt big and firm and ever so competent. She almost said no—she was tired—but her fingers felt so good, a warm aftertaste to the best thing she'd ever had, and she was tired, but—she needed it, needed more. Chaoua fingered her slowly, firmly, and cradled in the strong arms of the dryad she came again, screaming, sweating, senseless in her pleasure.

She gently slumped to the floor, spent, and Chaoua nestled onto her soft arm, her face against her breast. She felt warm and ecstatic and good from her toes to her cheeks. Their breathing slowed and synchronized. Ramona was almost—almost—asleep on the floor of the coffee shop behind the coffee counter when Chaoua stirred and stretched.

"Thank you," she said. "A thousand thanks."

Ramona smiled sleepily. "Thank you."

"I should go."

"I should too."

Chaoua sat up and stretched some more, so glossy and beautiful.

"If—if I can—may I come back and visit you?"

Ramona blushed deeply and sat up, her body humming still. "I would like that."

Ramona pulled on her clothes and Chaoua swept up the beans with her hands, setting them reverently into the bag. They finished their tasks and stood across from each other, neither willing to leave.

"I... can I walk you to the door?"

Chaoua put out her hand, and Ramona took it, and they opened the door together. The night was cool and fragrant with the smell of autumn leaves.

"Won't you be cold?" She touched Chaoua's shoulder, and it was still warm.

Chaoua laughed. "I am a being of the trees. We get cold, we get hot. We sleep, we wake, we grow." She leaned down—she was taller again, almost stretching to the height of the sapling oak outside the coffee house door—and kissed Ramona on the lips, gently, smelling for a second like hot, fresh espresso.

"I'll see you soon," Chaoua said.

"I look forward to it," Ramona whispered.

Chaoua let go of her hand and in a blink she wasn't there at all. Ramona gave a little gasp, and then saw something—something brown, something with wings, something a little textured, like bark—dart through the orange oak leaves and into the sky. Ramona held her breath and watched and waited, but that was it. Chaoua was gone.

Inside, Ramona's phone was ringing.

"Ramona?" It was Anne.

"Hey! I'm, um, almost done here." She blushed, though she did not feel bad at all.

"Great, thank you. I can't wait to try it out tomorrow." There was a pause. "Listen... I was wondering. Do you want to get a drink sometime?"

Ramona looked at the coffee flowers and breathed in the lingering scent of hot, wet espresso.

"Yeah. I'd like that."

Off the phone, she took a paper pastry bag and she filled it to the brim with perfect white flowers, and she took them home. She poured them into a bowl and watched as they slowly turned into beautiful red coffee cherries. Their husks died and, one day, fell off, and Ramona would run her fingers through the green coffee beans and breathe in their delicate scent, remembering.

Drink to Seal the Bond
Avery Vanderlyle

My last hope to claim my power lay inside the former warehouse on the outskirts of Winnipeg that housed the werecivet clan. I circled the building from a distance; my Changeling eyesight allowed me to see the details even in darkness. The peeling paint and cracks were artfully applied above layers of sturdy new wood. I could hear nothing from inside the building. Gleams of light shone between shutters on the second floor, but the ground floor was sealed up tight.

I wore a black men's suit. The somberness suited my mood; the androgyny suited my desire to appear inconspicuous. I had no idea if it was suited to the occasion. I was about to engage in a ritual that was only a rumor outside of were society.

I'd learned that the wereciv brewed a version of kopi luwak as a coming of age ritual. The young weres trespassed onto Fay land before taking their civet form. They grazed on any magical herbs they could pillage while eating the coffee fruits.

The resulting coffee beans were ground and the drink prepared on the dark of the moon, when landmarks are few, in vessels of virgin silver. Drinking the brew was the climax of this rite of passage. The fermentation that cured the coffee beans was an unpredictable magical process, while the other plants that were ingested added additional effects. Anything could happen to those who dared to drink. And the price for those few sips was high. But I was desperate.

It was time. I approached the entrance to the building. The man guarding it wrinkled his nose as I approached. A werecivet protecting his clan. He wore jeans and a black t-shirt with a gray sports jacket like any bouncer.

"Changeling," he hissed.

I was cast out from the Fay as an infant, ears cropped, and enchanted to pass for human, but the weres know.

"Yes," I replied. "If one of your initiates will accept me, I've come to drink the brew. I can offer a term of service."

"Nothing to offer but your skin, then." His eyes were piercing and feral in the dark.

I opened my mouth to muster a defense—I had skills—but he shrugged and stepped aside. I imagined whiskers twitching in a snouted face.

"Not my place to deny you," he rasped, motioning me forward. "Perhaps you'll find what you're looking for."

As I moved past him, he continued, "Perhaps you'll die."

"Changelings don't die easily." But his words prickled against the back of my neck as I opened the metal door.

The hallway was one story, here, closing in around me. Vapor billowed along the low ceiling. The bitter scent of coffee and the tang of musk rolled over me as I stepped forward. The short corridor was cold and dark. The wooden door a few meters in front of me must lead to the warehouse floor. The door was painted with vermilion runes: Warning. Destiny.

The outer door thudded shut behind me. Forward, then. My long strides took me to the inner door. I put my hand over the rune for Destiny and pushed.

The stench of animals rutting coated my throat. I gagged, overwhelmed by scents of urine, semen, civet oil. I pulled a breath in through my mouth and dashed water from my eyes as I adjusted to the scene.

On a pile of furs, a tangle of writhing figures fucked. Some were human, some I assumed changed weres, some in transition between forms. Gender preference and finesse had both been abandoned in service to an intoxicated pleasure. Is this what the brew did to those who drank?

A woman screamed, the sound piercing through the groans and grunts of the others. In glory or distress? I scanned the mass of figures, but couldn't find her. Dim gas lamps cast flickering lights that highlighted an arm, buttocks, a face in ecstasy. No one struggled to escape or reached for help.

"Second thoughts?"

I started and fell into a fighting stance, almost striking the young woman who stood before me.

She smiled, unafraid.

"I—" To survive I'd had to blend in. In the small town in New York state where I was raised, unobtrusiveness was a virtue.

Her smile grew cheeky. Her eyes glinted. "You are not for them, eh?" She glanced at the orgy. "I'm Ana. Maybe you're for me instead. Come."

She offered me her hand and I took it. Her grip was comforting and her skin soft. She had warm dark eyes, short shining black hair, skin like caramel.

We skirted the orgy and reached an area of settees and hookahs on low tables over Oriental rugs. Incense and tobacco mingled with the musk, moderating the smells of sex. But it was still more opium den than café. Men and women and people of indeterminate gender drank and smoked and laughed, ignoring the debauchery within arms' reach.

Above us, the open loft was ringed with a railed gallery. A few spectators leaned over the rails.

As we passed, a woman staggered out of the bacchanal to collapse into the arms of a couple lounging at one of the tables. They smiled and stroked her hair and teased her. She giggled, blushing, and hid her face against the woman's bosom.

Loneliness dug into my throat like a garrote. I'd been cast out because I had no Fay magic I could use. Instead, I had moments in which greater realities whirled around me, out of my reach, accompanied by seizures. If this ritual could bring me control of my magic, I could find a teacher and community with other Changelings.

Or perhaps both the seizures and the haunting glimpses of a

power I could never touch would be banished and I could find some peace in the human world.

Either way was worth the risk.

Past the settees were eight low tables, each with their own silver carafe lit by a golden flame. The scent of coffee dominated here, fruity with hints of cocoa and caramel. The musk lingered only in traces of warmth that settled deep in my gut as I breathed in. Beyond the tables twin staircases on the left and right rose up to meet the second floor gallery.

Ana led me to an unoccupied table. She dropped cross-legged onto the rug on the far side. "Sit." She smiled. "Breathe deep and relax. We'll talk. Bargain. Drink. What can I call you?"

"Lou. It's short for Louisa." I folded awkwardly onto the floor. The light created an island of security; we seemed miles away from the chaos at the entrance.

"I never heard of a Changeling wanting to drink the brew," she said. She leaned over the table. Her breasts were tight under a taupe silk top, her nipples prominent.

I tore my eyes away from her chest. I wasn't usually so obvious—

She grinned and looked me up and down. With all we'd traversed, my coyness was ridiculous.

"Lou, even if we could predict the brew's powers, we can't send you back to Fay lands."

"I know that."

"So what brings you here? Camilla had a vampire pay her 50,000 dollars to see if the brew would allow him to walk under the sun."

My heart jumped. If it could break one rule of nature, perhaps it could break others.

"Did it work?"

"We'll know for sure in the morning." She smirked. "We never had a vampire drink the brew before, either, but he is having a good time." She jerked her head back toward the front of the room.

"Is sex required?" My voice was hesitant but my cunt clenched. Away from the tumult, I could admit I wanted her.

"Sex is traditionally part of the bond between supplicant and brewer. But it can be private." Her eyes danced. "I don't think that'll be a problem for you."

"In private? No problem, Ana." Changelings do not blush, but my face itched as the skin tightened. I shifted up onto my knees.

Ana sat up to match me, assessing me.

"I have no magic. I have fits where the power shakes through me, but I can't use it. I've tried human epilepsy medicine. I've tried electric shock. Changeling charms from a dozen practitioners, herbal remedies from every tradition I could find. Nothing helps. I hope that either the brew will give me access to my power or take it all away. No more fits. I would be satisfied with either outcome."

"Those are possible. Not guaranteed." Ana wet her lips, and the urge to kiss her hissed through me like a snake.

"I understand. I accept the risk."

"Good. What do you have to offer in exchange for this, supplicant?"

"Brewer, in exchange I offer a term of service. Seven years is traditional." Her eyes widened and I rushed on. "I have black belts in karate and tae kwon do. I am well versed in other forms of hand-to-hand combat. I can fire a pistol. I can duel with a rapier—"

"You would make someone an admirable bodyguard." Ana frowned. "I don't need a bodyguard. I want to become a famous tattoo artist, not a gangster. I could use a business assistant for bookings, for marketing." Her eyes fell to my chest, then glanced lower. Her dark eyelashes caught the reflected gleam of the light. "I could also use a companion for more intimate purposes."

"What if we aren't well suited?" I wanted her, but I didn't know what spending years with someone would be like.

Her wide brown eyes met mine again. "I think we are. And

intent matters; the brew will see to it. Know that service is not slavery. But if you don't abide by our agreement, the magic will turn on you."

"I came prepared to make this promise."

"So you agree to my proposal?"

"To be your assistant and lover?" I took a breath, heart pounding. All my years of questing came to this moment. "I agree."

She bowed her head.

"Acknowledged, supplicant." She straightened and turned to the silver pot idling over the otherworldly gold flame. "The taking of the brew is our ancient custom. It contains traces of the intimate journey the coffee beans went through as well as the uncontrolled Fay magic that will bind us. I hope you get what you wish."

She poured the dark liquid into a small silver cup. The rich aroma rose around us. I breathed deep again.

"Tell me about the journey to make this coffee, Ana."

Ana cradled the cup in both hands. "There were ten of us. We dashed past the Fay sentries into the Hill's herb gardens. I ate my coffee fruits, relishing the sweet pulp and swallowing the seeds. We dove into the gardens, feasting on Devil's Bit, teasel, marshmallow root, and saffron. We dared a bite of mandrake and breathed in the scent of the rose gardens. Then the Fay released their hounds to hunt us and we raced for the portal...."

She closed her eyes. "Two of my friends were trapped in the Fay enclave where we trespassed. One of the hounds snapped so close to me he yanked a jawful of fur off my leg."

"In my experience, power and danger are always intertwined."

She opened her eyes and stared into mine. "Then you are better prepared for this moment that most." She raised the cup above her head. "I drink to honor the memory of those who didn't return. I drink to honor the Brewer and the Supplicant, the ritual going back millennia."

She lowered the cup and took a sip of the coffee. "I drink to set the bond." She handed me the cup. "Drink to seal the bond."

The silver was warm in my cupped hands. I breathed in the

scent, warm and complex. Highlights of berry and butter and brown sugar made my mouth water. Hints of rose and the bitterness of mandrake teased at my senses.

"I drink to seal the bond."

I took a sip. As coffee goes, it was mild, the taste muted compared to the scent, with whispers of marshmallow and saffron adding sweetness and richness to the brew. But I wasn't drinking it for the flavor.

"The bond is sealed," Ana said. "Drink the rest."

"Thank you." Anything could happen, but I wanted her to know I appreciated the chance. I drained the cup, the warmth of the coffee mixing with the heat of desire to kindle my blood.

She grinned. "I like you. The brew intensifies desire, so let's go to my room before the magic solidifies." Ana rose, quick and graceful as a wild cat. She held out her hand. "Come."

I rose, capturing her smooth fingers in mine, and brushed my lips across the back of her hand.

She shivered. The same shudder struck me. I stepped closer to her, craving to hold her. My hands slid up her arms and across her slender shoulders as our lips met.

The taste of the coffee lingered in her mouth, more potent there than in the cup. How much of this lust overwhelming me was the magic? How much the desire that had been creeping through me since she first took my hand?

Her lips pressed harder. Her breasts crushed against mine as I pulled her close. She moaned a little, tongue flicking in my mouth. Then she pushed against me, pulling away. "Unless the fire in you calls you to the orgy, come with me."

She took a step back, out of my arms, hands extended. When I reached to grab them she pulled away, taking another step back. Ana grinned and dashed to the staircase.

I could play that game. A Changeling can move faster than a were, even in the dark. My arms went around her waist and I pulled her close. She went limp, warm and supple. Her ass wiggled against my crotch playfully.

"Which room is yours?" I growled in her ear.

"Second one on the right at the top of the stairs." She gasped, breathless.

My blood heated. I picked her up and tossed her over my shoulder. Her startled shriek morphed into peals of laughter. I carried her up to the gallery, then to her door.

❀

Ana's room had a futon with silk sheets on the floor next to a fire-place that held a huge, flickering candle. I caught a glimpse of a wooden chest, a half-empty bookcase, a sketchpad. Ana slid onto the futon and pulled her shirt off, and nothing else mattered.

Her small taut breasts and dark nipples made my mouth water. I dropped to my knees and bent to taste.

Her skin tasted like marshmallow. As I sucked her breasts, she undid my trousers, shoving them and my underwear down my thighs. She moaned, then laughed when she found me wet already.

Her slender fingers slipped inside me, caressing and probing. Her thumb brushed my clit lightly, and the pleasure surged. I gasped.

I switched my mouth from her left breast to her right. A fresh rush of sweetness burst over my tongue. Her fingers pushed and pressed and brushed, and I came. Pushing her fingers deeper, growling around her nipple, I writhed against the silk. Pleasure drowned me; I foundered like a boat in heavy seas.

When the rush faded, I realized her breast was still in my mouth. I licked at it again, feeling her shiver.

I lifted my head to see her smiling. Her skin gleamed in the candlelight.

"Lou." She stretched, arching her back so her breasts caught the light. "Take all your clothes off."

As I obeyed, I felt Ana's lust in a wave of heat against my skin. Was this the bond between us, or my imagination?

Eyes locked with mine, her fingers shimmied her skirt down her strong legs. She kicked off her shoes and spread herself open for me. It was an honor to lower myself between her legs and bring my mouth in to her. I licked her clit and nuzzled at her folds.

Sweetness from marshmallow and the honey-salt of saffron surrounded me: on my tongue, drawn deep in my lungs with each breath. Ana's hands caught in my short hair as my tongue burrowed deeper. She moaned as I licked and sucked and kissed her. Nectar flowed into my mouth and coated my chin.

Ana didn't have to tell me where to go, hard or soft, up or down, because I felt it like a magnet tugs a compass needle.

When she came, moans rising into cries, her pleasure surged over me so strongly I couldn't tell if I had my own orgasm as well or merely absorbed hers.

And with the ebb of ecstasy, joyful satiation flowed into me.

"Ana, do you feel...."

"What you feel?" Her smile was blissful. "I think it's the bond. Making sure we take good care of each other."

How could I regret that? I crawled up her body to kiss her.

Pressed together, I could feel her thoughts, not just her emotions: A bargain well struck. Surprise at what the fates had given her. Hope that this arrangement would give her the partner she'd lacked.

That last thought was so close to what I'd hoped for.

So I kissed her harder, savoring the returned press of her lips and tongue. I felt her nipples harden as desire flared between us again.

I sat up to trail fingers down her breast. Sparks danced in front of my eyes that weren't from the candlelight. The world tilted and started to spin.

"Oh, no." I tried to force it away.

"Lou." Her hands gripped mine.

"I hoped this would be over," I ground out. I pitched off her as the fit took me. My fingers slipped in the silk as the world spun and shattered. Past, present, future—not just our world but other worlds—all jumbled together.

I was standing inside a vortex while the three Fay magics whipped around me: the Other worlds, Insight into the future, and glimpses of the Pattern that drove all existence. Aspects of each whirled around, shiny and dark like fragments of obsidian, incomprehensible and out of reach. The air was heavy with ozone and unnaturally still as it always was when I hovered in the eye of the storm.

But tonight, with the magical brew inside me, I had to try. I reached out into the vortex. For the first time in my life, I could touch it! A fragment slid across my palm, oily and wriggling. I closed my fist around a hunk that oozed through my fingers. Gone. I grabbed for something else; it sliced into my palm. A drizzle of my blood spun out into the whirlwind.

I tried again. I grasped a piece, tarnish veined with silver that wriggled like a fish in my grip. I pulled it free and held it against my chest.

The totem leached into me and I saw the future: the vampire would walk in the sun for a few minutes, but the ability would fade before he noticed and he would wither into dust.

I was shaking, sweating, my muscles weak as if I'd run a marathon. But I had gained one moment of Insight! I laughed in triumph and reached out again. I clutched greedily, seizing whatever I could:

A gray jagged hunk yielded a path to a world, lush and green, with a Fay castle amid formal gardens. Going there would be death for a Changeling.

The next totem, marbled and pocked like a sponge, led to a world inhabited only by wyverns and stout, dark dwarves—a world that was not forbidden. The map to it filled my mind.

I pulled free a long sliver, drops of fluid welling up on its surface. It wrapped around me and part of the Pattern was revealed. War between the humans and the Fay, forgotten in human memory, would come again. Already the troops were assembling....

I reeled and stumbled back, trying to escape the knowledge. The vortex reached out for me. It had never done that before. It grabbed. I flailed at it, my training useless against chaos itself. My heart pounded as I pulled my arms in, dropping to a crouch, centering myself and imagining a floor under me.

If I got sucked in I would unravel.

I really could die.

As I straightened, the vortex shrunk tighter around me. I could see the shapes of the elements within it now, shining like patches of oil in the sun.

I felt a surge of concern from outside me. Ana. I could feel her even here. I wasn't alone. My stance strengthened with her feelings anchoring me.

The elements within the vortex slapped at me with slimy appendages, whipping sodden tails across my face. Could I grasp the right tools to tame the vortex before it overwhelmed me? If I didn't succeed—and soon—I would be overpowered and destroyed!

I was already exhausted.

The other choice was to banish the vortex altogether. I had made a solemn pact with Ana and the power of the brew surged within me. I could give up on the magic, live among the weres and forge a new life for myself.

I closed my eyes and focused on Ana's fear and blossoming affection. It was easy. The way out glowed in my mind like rungs of a ladder.

Eyes still closed, I reached up and felt the solid bar under my hands. I pulled myself up, arms shaking. The vortex closed in, slime dripping down my back. It stank of manure and tainted oil. I couldn't breathe, but I reached for Ana's presence and kept on.

Covered, smothered, I heaved myself up another rung. My arms burned as if I'd climbed a sheer cliff. The chaos clung to me, thickening like molasses. Hints of the power it could bring whispered against my mind.

Lies. I couldn't control it. I clambered up one more step.

Something warm and firm touched my face. I hauled myself up another rung and the air was fresh and clear. I took a deep breath. The vortex dissolved, a few last wisps sliding around my ankles before they faded away.

I shuddered. Another warm pat on my cheek and I opened my eyes.

My head was cradled in Ana's lap as we lay naked in the

sheets. I was trembling with exhaustion, but the vortex was gone. I was home.

"I grasped a few bits of knowledge, but then it turned on me." I struggled to sit up. "The vampire—we have to warn him—"

"We will." Ana touched my lips. "It turned on you but you defeated it."

I nodded. "I think it's banished for good," I whispered.

Ana pushed the hair away from my forehead. "If it comes back I'll be here to help you fight it."

"I'm not tempted anymore. The bond is enough."

She smiled. "Yes, it is."

Her fingers brushed my cheek a third time and I caught her hand in mine.

Flavor Profile of a Smuggler
Rebecca Croteau

I saw her long before she saw me. She was tall, willowy, hair an orange sort of red, a mass of curls that reached halfway down her back. She swayed with movements of the station that I hadn't noticed in twenty years.

Her eyes passed over me without any sign of notice. Silly smuggler. She should have identified me before she even stepped into the cafe. To be fair, she looked as wet behind the ears as they come at this job, and she was probably looking for someone with blue skin and a Fed's star worn right on their lapel. It wouldn't occur to a newbie to look for a Terran, and one with brown skin and braids to her shoulders at that.

I watched her as I lifted my cup of koffee to my lips. I told myself it was fine, just like the stuff I remembered from Earth Prime when I was a little kid. It hadn't worked yet.

They'd had to modify the genetics of the plant quite a lot to get it to grow on the farm worlds we'd Terraformed. Something about the soil needs or the air quality. Technically, the two plants tasted exactly the same. But the koffee had always lacked something to me. Maybe it was the romance of childhood. I'd drunk proper café in my grandmère's kitchen in New Orleans. It had been paired with homemade beignets and mellowed out with pure cream. And it had been made by Grandmère. Nothing else was going to measure up to it. The experts assured me that was the only reason that I, and the couple other billion people who had long since stopped being able to afford real coffee from Earth Prime, didn't like its cousin.

I turned my attention back to the girl. She looked to be in her twenties, so at least she was old enough to be legally off planet.

That would avoid an hour's paperwork at least. She looked clean. Her hair was pulled back from her face, and her clothing, while typical leather and denim outlaw wear, looked like it was fresh and new. Odds were good that a quick scan would find her ID in the system for me, no drama. This was going to be an easy nab, and would cement my new position with the Nymatao, the blue-skinned tentacled aliens who owned this station. They'd decided that having a Terran security force would be good for business. I needed the money, if I was ever going to get back down to the planet and reopen Grandmère's little cafe.

I watched her, and I waited for her to do something that would confirm that I was right about her intentions.

For all that the way she studied the crowd in the cafe seemed fresh and new, her stance was professional and careful. I watched her survey the staff and the bar, and when she finally chose a seat, it was in the section served by a woman that I too would have judged as sympathetic to her cause. As she walked across the floor, she put a little extra sashay into her walk. I didn't mind that, to tell the truth and shame the devil.

She was smooth with her hands; she passed her credit to the server along with a slim note that I wouldn't have noticed if I hadn't been specifically looking for it. The server took it without looking down. Interesting. That was something I'd have to look into later; most people would check to see what was in their hand reflexively.

The server passed the note to Garill, who opened it, glanced down at it, and then met my gaze. The sharp little nod he gave me was all I was waiting for. Unfortunately, she was looking for it too, and she hit her feet at the same time that I did. She was fast, hitting full speed by the time she got to the door, and she had a wingman I hadn't noticed—drag it—who stumbled in front of me, slowing me down just long enough that I wasn't sure which way she went outside the bar. I pushed the stumbler out of my way and rushed out the door. I looked left, right, center—and didn't see her anywhere. The ring was busy, but I didn't see a break in the flow of the crowd.

I cursed out loud and turned to go back inside the cafe and see what Garill had to say for himself.

Garill had less information than I'd hoped. He insisted that his server's skill with subterfuge was something she'd picked up prior to her employment with him, and he'd make sure to address the issue with her. The note was vague; it made clear that the girl had something to sell, but it wasn't enough to stand up in court, not even the Fed courts. She could argue that she was just trying to sell something she'd grown or made herself, a new blend for a tisane. Without a clear indication of the smuggled item, or being found with the actual contraband, the courts wouldn't bother with her.

I knew there was more going on.

I doubted she'd leave the station; she didn't look like she had enough experience to know when she needed to cut and run. The odds were high she'd just try another cafe, maybe on a different ring.

I went back to my quarters and changed my clothes, swapping out the casual slacks I wore for work, and found a long, velvety skirt in bright blue that was slit up to my thigh, and a flowing linen blouse in a light gray that brushed my curves when I moved. My braids went from hanging back loose from my face to being twisted into an updo. The effect changed from security force to wealthy traveler. If she was as inexperienced as I thought, than she might try to sell whatever she had to a private purchaser, figuring it was less hassle and less traceable than selling to a Fed subsidized operation.

I wandered the station. I didn't stay too long in any one place, and I tried not to make much of an impression anywhere I went. Just a ghost, wandering through, invisible and intangible.

It wasn't long before I found her. She was talking heatedly to a Gavrokin behind the bar, and he was shaking his mandibles furiously. "No," I heard him hiss in agitated tones. "I cannot. I am sorry for your family. I wish you no harm. But I cannot risk my own family. You understand?"

"No," she replied, I heard the tremble of a much younger girl in her voice, though her eyes were hard as titanium. "No, I don't understand."

The Gavrokin shifted its mandibles aggressively. I took my moment to intercede.

I put my hands on her shoulders, gave the purple insectoid a smile, and steered her away from the bar. "Let's sit down," I murmured to her, although I didn't think she heard me, with all the tears sliding from her eyes. She followed me demurely enough, though.

I sat us down in the corner of the bar, where darkness shielded us from prying gazes. "My name's Lia," I said, stroking her hand. "Tell me what's happening. Perhaps I can help."

She was in tears, her face shielded in her hands. I sighed and waved down a server, asking for two cups of koffee, pale and sweet. They were on the table quickly enough. I pushed one toward the girl, who sighed, wiped her eyes, took a sip—and then sprayed hot brown liquid over the table and me. "What in the name of God was that?"

I raised an eyebrow and made a show of wiping the drips off my blouse. "Koffee," I said. "Surely you've had it before? Gaz is far from the best brewmaster I've ever known, but he's not that bad."

"That's disgusting swill," she said, wiping at her mouth with a napkin. At least she wasn't crying any more. "Sorry about your shirt. I've just... that was awful."

"You get used to it," I said. I was adding up two and two and getting mighty close to four. "You've never had it before, have you? The modified stuff you get off planet?"

Her gaze was steady, but her eyes were becoming nervous. "I'm not sure what you mean. I've never lived on Earth."

I kept my smile easy as I took a sip out of my cup. "I don't think that's true. I think you're up here because your family is on the brink of some sort of disaster, so you got your hands on something to sell, and you thought you'd peddle it directly, because the Feds take a huge cut, and everyone knows it. That about right?"

I could see the war in her soft, dark eyes. She wanted to tell me the truth in case I could help; she was smart enough to know that every person she told was one more chance to be exposed. And the Feds were not kind to smugglers.

A normal person would probably feel guilty for entrapping her like this. I probably would have, too. Once upon a time.

"Not here," she said, finally. "Where can we go?"

I gave her a smile, smooth and interested, as much for anyone watching as for her. "My quarters are on this ring. Will that be secure enough for you?"

She gave a quick nod, and when I stood, she followed me.

"This is lovely," Shan said, spinning in a circle and surveying the living area of my quarters. "All the other rooms I've seen have felt so spartan, so cold. This feels like a home."

"It is my home," I said, sinking down onto the sofa and relaxing. "What did you want to show me?"

She reached into the bag she wore over her shoulder. As soon as she pulled out the silver air-seal canister, I knew exactly what was in it. I tried to keep my expression neutral, but I knew without doubt that I was failing miserably. My eyes were wide, my lips parted. "Is that—"

She nodded, her lips turned up in the smallest smile. "Have you ever?"

"Not in twenty years," I said.

There was more confidence in her walk as she crossed the small space of my floor. She sat down next to me, just as artful in her leather as I was in linen and velvet. She held the canister close to my nose before she cracked it open.

The smell was like nothing else. Like the earth on a warm day, like spices lightly toasted over a fire, like fruit ripening in the sun. I had to swallow the rush of saliva and fight back memories of Grandmère smiling as she urged me to drink up.

"Oh my god," I murmured, and she smiled.

"I can make you a cup," she said, moving the canister gently so that the fragrance of the coffee spread gently on the air.

"And you would sell me this?"

She nodded.

"Name your price."

She leaned forward, her fingertips brushing the side of my breast as she whispered a number—a ridiculously low number that told me she had no idea of the value of the item off planet— into my ear. She backed off a bit so I could see her face, and she smiled, her lips parted in invitation. I couldn't help but kiss her.

Her lips were incredibly soft, exceedingly delicate. Her kiss was tentative, but there was passion behind it. I took the canister of coffee and closed it carefully, setting it on the floor, then took both her hands in mine. I pushed them up above her head, pressing her back into the arm of my sofa. She sighed, shifting underneath me. "Yes," she whispered. "Oh, please. You're lovely, yes, please."

It made it so much harder to say the words. "Shannon Marie McLaine, you are bound under the authority of the Earth Prime Federation for suspicion of trafficking illegal goods." The energy cuffs snapped around her hands, locking them together in a powerful binding. She yanked them down into her lap, pulling furiously at the cuffs as I settled back, trying to calm my racing heart.

I should have called immediately to have her transported to holding. Or taken her there myself. I knew that. I wasn't sure what was keeping me still on the couch? The coffee in its canister, or the growing look of calculation in her eyes. She shifted on the cushions, letting her leather-clad thighs hiss against each other. "I know this looks bad," she said.

I reached over and brushed my finger over her lip to shush her. She pouted, then flicked her tongue over the pad of my finger, and I had to choke back a sigh.

"You don't want to do this, Lia," she said. "You'd already be taking me to holding, if that's what you wanted. But it's not enough to just smell it, is it? You want a taste." She caressed the word, her eyes locked on mine. "Do you even remember how to make it, anymore?"

I shook my head. When I was growing up, coffee was expensive, though it wasn't anything like was now. Grandmère always made it herself, even when I was a teenager. "It would cost me a year's pay to buy a single cup," I said. "You know that. I can't buy this from you, and I need to turn you in."

"Is it me you're convincing, or yourself?"

"I need my job. I need to be able to get back down to Prime. The land is still in my name, but without proper papers, I'm not allowed on land anymore."

"My family has been growing coffee for generations," she said. "In the beginning, we got to keep a portion of the crop for ourselves. The portion has been getting smaller and smaller over the years, as the market prices got higher and higher, and more and more beans were siphoned off for political bribes and black market purchases. And then my father was caught with a single cup. They took us off our land." She gestured towards the canister. "That's all I could salvage of our final crop. If I can sell it, my family will have enough money to at least support my parents. So perhaps we can work something out?"

"There's nothing to work out." My tone was far harsher than I meant it to be, but her only response was to narrow her eyes. "I'm sorry about your family, but I can't help you."

"One cup," she said. "One cup for my freedom." The wheedling, flirtatious tone was gone from her voice.

"I can't." I put as much force and emotion into those two words as I could. The button to call transport was conveniently located right by the entrance to my suite. Why hadn't I pressed it yet? "I can't."

She shifted again, taking my measure. "What if I sweeten the deal?"

I didn't move as she leaned towards me. Her lips pressed down onto mine again, but there was no tentative, delicate motion this time. This kiss had a goal, and I was it. Her tongue traced over my lower lip, and I opened myself to her. She teased at my lower lip with her teeth, stroked into my mouth with her tongue.

"I can't set you free," I said one more time.

"Let me touch you." Her bound hands came up together, brushing over my breasts, taunting my nipples. "I want to touch you."

It had been so long. There were only so many temptations I could resist in one short evening. I wrapped my hands around the energy cuffs, and twisted them into release position.

She didn't waste time. Her hands parted the linen of my blouse, freeing my breasts from their binding, and bringing them to her tongue. Her teeth teased delicately at my nipples, and the first swirls of excitement began to coil in the lowest bits of my belly.

"May I undress you?" She kissed lower down on my belly, nipping at my navel and making me whimper.

"Please." My voice was a thin thread dragged out of me by her fingers.

She stood, pulling me to my feet. I let her ease my blouse over my shoulders, drop my skirt and my panties to the floor. I stood naked before her as she added her own leathers to the pile.

She was utterly gorgeous. Her body was soft and curved, but under the sweet swells and waves, she had the sort of muscle that is earned through hard, repetitive labor. Her skin was paler than I'd ever thought a farmer would be able to keep it, especially in the regions where coffee grew well. She hesitated for a moment then, her eyes suddenly nervous. They flicked up to mine. I had the oddest sense that she was seeking approval for her nakedness.

I opened my arms, and she stepped into them eagerly enough, turning her face up towards mine. The kiss was more even now in power, our tongues tangled together. My hands came to her hair, and hers to my ass. It was my turn to make her whimper as I bore down on her mouth, turning her head to give me the angle I wanted. She pulled me back down onto the couch, my weight on top of her. Her knees spread, letting my thigh come between them. Her cunt was burning hot as she pressed herself up into my thigh, her eyes wide, her pupils huge in her bright eyes. It hadn't been a long time just for me.

I bent my head down, taking the pale brown circle of her nipple into my mouth, teasing it with my teeth as she had done. Her entire body tensed as she hissed with need. "Fingers," she whimpered. "Touch me."

I'd never been one to refuse a command from a beautiful woman. I slipped my hand down between her thighs, circling her clit for a few moments while she hissed and bucked until I slid a bit further down, letting my fingers fill her deeply. She groaned, her hands flying over my body and hers, meeting the thrusts of my fingers with her arching hips.

She came fast and hard and sudden, her teeth biting at her lip, her body tight and silent and throbbing around my fingers.

She took no time to relax or enjoy the delight. She growled, pushing me backwards, parting my thighs with her hands and burying her face against my sex. Her tongue sought out my clit as her fingers quested farther back, teasing into my ass. I groaned, the sensations tightening and swirling too quickly, too rapidly. She pushed me into an orgasm before I had a chance to properly enjoy it, and it was lovely to feel my pussy pulsing under her tongue, it had been so long—but she didn't stop when I thought she would, instead pushing harder, faster, moving her thumb to my clit to swirl and circle while she entered me with her tongue, plunging to the depths of me, tasting me thoroughly.

The aftershocks hadn't even ended when I was coming again, bursting and shattering in her hands. She brought me again and again in those few moments, my body shredding itself with delight until I was finally, deeply, truly sated.

She kissed me, her chin and mouth soaked with my sex and

my scent. I kissed her, my hand resting lightly on her hair. "Thank you," I said. "You're amazing."

She smiled. "I'll make you that cup now," she said, settling back and reaching for her leather pants on the floor.

Free of her weight, I stood. I don't know how she knew; did I give it away in that moment, or had she suspected the entire time? If she was surprised when I crossed the floor, my breasts swaying, and pressed the button that would summon the Fed team, she hid it well. She pulled her clothes back on, then held out her wrists. I locked them together before slipping into my skirt and blouse again. "I did warn you," I said.

"That you did."

"The story about your family was good, though. I almost believed you."

The door to my chamber opened, and two uniformed guards entered. I passed them the canister. "What gave me away?" she asked.

I shrugged, keeping my expression cold and neutral. "That would be telling secrets."

Her smile was cold, her cheeks still flushed from her orgasm. She didn't speak again as the guards took her out of the room. I assured them that I'd be down in the morning to file my report. She'd be gone already, on her way to a prison world. Of course, the cuffs I'd used were only really good for one reliable hold. A second one was liable to fail after just a few minutes. She might know that; she might not. She might get free; she might not. It was the best chance I could give her.

I couldn't sleep.

I tossed and turned, chasing phantom hands and soft kisses. I twisted my hands in the sheets as my thighs squeezed together, and when I couldn't stand it anymore, I let my fingers slip between my lower lips and rubbed out two hard, fast, utilitarian orgasms that only made me want her more and again. I could see her green eyes staring down into mine as I came for her, again and again.

I gave up after a time. I showered, twisted my braids up out of the way, and dressed. My shift wouldn't actually start for another hour, but I'd be able to get my report done and filed, and maybe then I'd be able to stop thinking about her.

I was nearly done with the written portion when Sagral, the Nymatao director of security, entered my cubicle. Unlike most of her kind, she shunned the translators they used, feeling that they were a lazy solution. When in Earth's orbit, she spoke our "Terran jabber." And couldn't grasp why we found the description offensive.

"You did well," Sagral said, carefully speaking her words through her nest of tentacles. "Good. Promotion coming for you, I think. Soon."

"Thank you," I said, forcing a smile onto my face. "What will happen to the girl?"

Sagral shrugged, an expression that was infinitely more interesting when the one making it had a dozen appendages capable of the motion. "Above my paygrade. Prison planet, I imagine. Your kind is not gentle with smugglers, even when they first offend."

My stomach twisted at the thought. Her story about her family had been a pile of shite, I felt sure of that, but there was something there. Life as a black market smuggler was less glamorous than most kidlets believed, and odds were that something had led her to this life.

Sagral patted my shoulders with her tentacles. I'd been here long enough that I'd lost the urge to shudder. "You did well. Not all see. You enjoy day off. Get sleep. You look—" She made a sound that sounded a bit like a dog vomiting. I couldn't have reproduced it, but I got the point.

I made my vid recording and headed back to my quarters. Exhaustion had hit like a truck, and I thought this time that no pretty green eyes would keep me awake.

I didn't turn the light on when I walked into my quarters. I couldn't turn off the emergency lights around the edges of the room, but I didn't need more than that to navigate. I went to my room, my head aching. I pulled off my shirt and reached for my binding.

"Keep going, Fed woman," a voice said in the darkness, and I jumped, my hand going for the stunner I hadn't carried since I lived on Prime. Old habits. A light flicked on in the darkness.

It took me a moment to recognize Shan in the darkness. "I thought you were on your way to prison." It was a tacky thing to say, but I'd reach for anything in that moment to cover my surprise.

Shan smiled, that bright and easy smile I'd seen in the bar. "Still behind, huh? That's all right. I'm off in a few minutes, I just— wanted to stop by and give you a present. Two, actually. If you're willing."

"Sure," I said, not sure what else to say. "Why not?"

She crossed the floor like a stroke of lightning, sweeping me into her arms, kissing me hard and fast and furious. I melted into her, letting her press me back down onto the bed. I rolled with her, letting her put me on top of her hips, and as I rocked over her, my body lighting on fire, I felt the hard length of the cock she wore now.

The look that crossed my face must have been like that of a child who has first seen the stars. "Yes," she whispered. "That is your first present. Do you want it?"

"I do," I murmured back, rocking against her again.

She stripped my pants, and hers. "How?" she murmured, nipping at my breasts again, stirring up that ache that I hadn't been able to settle all night long.

"Like this?" I whimpered as I rolled onto my hands and knees. "It hasn't been like this in so long."

"Oh, yes," she said, and slapped my ass hard enough to sting. I was wet, but still tight, and as the tip of her cock pressed against me, I groaned all the way down to my toes. She pushed into me so delicately, so softly. I cried out, electric pleasure twirling around my clit already, driving me to distraction. Each thrust pushed her just a little further into me until I'd taken all of her. I steadied my body, ready for her to find a speed and a push that drove us both crazy, but instead, she kept her movements slow and steady. She dragged over the nubbled place deep inside me that could push me over the edge so quickly, but the softness of her strokes left me yearning, crying out in soft tones, throbbing around her, begging her for more, and faster, and harder.

She paid no attention to my begging, just kept fucking me slow and steady until I thought I'd die from the pleasure that wouldn't burst.

And then she ran her finger around my soft, soaked pussy, collecting the moisture that was spilling from me with each whimpery little cry. I knew what was coming, but I still wasn't prepared for the intensity of the sensation as she slid that one finger into my ass again.

Before, everything had been so fast, so intense. Now, my entire body felt like it was breaking open under her tender ministrations. She worked her finger and her cock into me, pulling one out as the other pushed in, keeping me always full of something.

When I came, the sensation was overwhelming to the extreme. I screamed into my mattress as she pulsed at me, short strokes that worked over the most attentive spots in my body; I started to come down, and my hard and aching nipples dragged over the rough cotton of my sheets, and I screamed again while she chucked softly, running her hand down my spine.

The second present was a surprise. I'd taken my turn, devoured her, made her cry out twice, her thighs wrapped around my head as she came for me. I'd buried my tongue in her ass while I stroked her cock, and she loved it, begging me to do it again and again. We laid tangled together for a bit, and then she got out of my bed and walked naked into the kitchen. I liked how her ass moved when she walked. It wasn't quite a sashay, definitely less than a shimmy, but more than a sway. It was her. It was Shan. I knew nothing about her, but I liked how she fucked, and how her ass moved.

She waved a much smaller air-seal canister at me that she'd

pulled out of one of the many pockets of her leather pants. I stood and followed her, my hands on those gorgeous hips, watching as she went through the familiar motions. Grinding the beans. Heating the water. Pouring it carefully over the grinds, then letting the water slowly make its way through the filter. I licked her neck and kissed her earlobe, smelling sex on the air and the fragrant, earthy smell of the coffee.

Shan turned back to me with one delicate cup held high. "May we meet again in better times," she said. "Not all of my story was a lie."

I nodded. "I didn't know if I was going to turn you in until the end."

"It's for the best that you did," she said.

I let the coffee roll over my tongue, mixing with her spicy flavors to make a blend I suspected I'd never have again.

It was five years before I saved enough to get my documentation, and get back to Prime. Two years after that to get Bon Temps back to something that approached operating standards. Two years more before her shadow filled my doorway.

"All the cafes in all the world, and you have to wander into mine," I whispered to myself. And then, louder. "What in the world are you doing here?"

Shannon Marie MacLaine sent my digital pad a set of credentials. "I heard you're looking for a Brewmaster," she said. "I thought I could help."

I saw quite a history on the document she'd produced. Years of service on a coffee plantation, but more than that, years of service to the Feds, paying off a debt. She'd helped to capture officers who'd looked the other way on black market sales. She'd seen several dozen illegally operating officers sent off into the black. "Interesting."

"Cup of coffee? If you don't mind?"

I nodded. "The beignet is on the house."

One Mocha, with Enchantment
K.L. Noone

The lines weren't right, Nate decided, staring at his sketch. Not wrong, but not right either. The coffee-mug was there, pencil-drift curves and a swirl of steam drifting along the page. The corner of the table was there, knotholes and weathered wood and all. But he couldn't feel it. Not the way he wanted to, as if he could taste darkly roasted beans and playful cream just by looking.

He sighed. Flipped the pencil idly across his fingers. Back and forth.

Behind the counter, skillful hands busy dusting a frothy confection with nutmeg, Gavin paused to radiate worry in his direction. Nate made a face at him, because that was the only appropriate response to overt concern from one's retired-deity present-day boyfriend, and although Gavin didn't say anything the coffee-mug warmed up again in its spot on the table.

Little things. Heat suffusing unbreakable ceramic, pouring into his palms. The way Gavin smiled at him sometimes, sideways and astonished, which was ridiculous because only one of them had once crafted bronze and silver weapons for fellow gods, and that one of them certainly wasn't Nate.

When he took a sip, the renewed warmth felt like a kiss.

In theory he'd been trying to work on the next illustrated children's book. More accurately this process had so far consisted of glaring at blank white pages and failing to have any decent ideas. He'd gone through three cappuccinos and far too many chocolate-pumpkin scones and pathetic gestures in the direction of inspiration via abandoned sketches of coffee-mugs, the pastry case, the dangling mismatched antique lamps overhead. Those lamps splashed calm topaz light over the café, an oasis in reverse, while the rain chuckled to itself outside.

Gavin finished performing complicated magic with the

gleaming mystery of the espresso machine, said something cheerful and incomprehensibly Gaelic to today's purple-haired pixie-faced assistant—she looked human, which didn't necessarily mean a thing—and wandered out from behind the counter. "Mo grá thú, and are you having difficulties?"

"Love you too, and absolutely yes." He put down the pencil in favor of reaching for the closest scarred hand. Those scars carried stories. He knew some of them. Knew about blacksmith's forges and battles on emerald-mist hillsides and the ache of sending men to kill and die. Knew there were more stories he didn't know. "Just not... feeling it, today."

"Hmm. Are you thinking about the Arthur book?"

"No," Nate said, which was only about half untrue. The Arthur book—*Legends of the Round Table*, his first illustrated book—had sold a truly staggering number of copies and picked up a few not unprestigious awards. Most reviews had praised the quirky dreamlike nature of the artwork, likening it to Arthur Rackham and the school of Brian Froud, commenting that he'd been unafraid to show the eerie nature of a true realm on the edge of Faerie.

All those reviewers and readers and audiences were waiting to see what he'd do next. So many eyes. Expectant.

"Yes," Gavin agreed, and stole his cappuccino, taking a sip. "Not at all. I can tell."

"You're a god. That's cheating. Also thank you."

"For what? And I can't read your mind. For the five hundredth time. Possibly one of my uncles could've, but I'm reading your face."

A line of deeper emotion lay under the teasing, familiar as the scents of cocoa and caffeine but less cozy. Those uncles, along with most of Gavin's family, were long gone, if not dead then someplace beyond any mortal comprehension. Assuredly not here in this scruffy-literary corner of Boston, at any rate.

"For being here," Nate said, and reclaimed his cappuccino. "For this. How do you do that one, anyway?"

"I ask the universe nicely. People tend to forget I was also a god of hospitality. Protection of all sorts." Gavin traced a finger over the battered old wood of the table. It looked like happily rescued salvage from a shipwreck. It was. The rescue'd taken place several hundred years previously. "I didn't only provide more efficient means for people to kill their own relations."

"Hey," Nate said, and put a hand on his wrist, thumb landing deliberately over one particular scar, "I know. I know, remember?" Even gods weren't immune to their own swords, or to anguish. And Gavin had been very tired, and very alone, once before.

That'd happened long before they'd ever met. And even knowing that, knowing he was here and able to be touched now, Nate would never not want to go back in time and hold him then.

"I know you do." Pale blue eyes followed the thumb as it rubbed assurance over silver-lined skin. Looking up, Gavin added, "I'm sorry. *Tá brón orm.* You were trying to work; can I help?"

"I was failing to work," Nate pointed out, and their eyes caught across lazy shimmering cinnamon-topped steam. Behind Gavin's back, the purple-haired possible pixie chattered at customers. The rain rustled down contentedly beyond the door, enclosing them and the café and the bookshelf-lined walls and the laptop-wielding residents in silver.

They'd met two years and three months and six days ago precisely. It'd been raining then too, and Nate had left his umbrella at the restaurant during lunch with his agent, bought another one, promptly left that one in a very distracting bookshop, and ducked into the nearest coffee-shop when the raindrops threatened to become hammers.

The café'd been equally homelike that afternoon. Overstuffed chairs and an eclectic collection of genuine historic artifacts—a spear, a battered cauldron, a bronze ring, a few remnants of folklore—decorating the walls. Modern wi-fi and for some reason a collection of nineteen-eighties rock ballads playing softly in the background. Bon Jovi, singing soulfully about livin' on a prayer.

Nate, dripping like a sheepdog and wondering how he'd managed to get *that* much water on his jeans in the course of two blocks, had looked up and found raven-wing dark hair and broad shoulders and startled winter-sky eyes looking at him.

He'd found out later, in bits and pieces, that the fluid black ink along Gavin's right bicep was a running pooka, a wild faerie-horse; that retired gods could sing Bon Jovi just as badly as anyone else; that half the regular clientele was more or other than human in varyingly noticeable ways. "They need someplace," Gavin had said, shutting the door on an unruly banshee who'd refused to stop shrieking that she needed more caffeine. The general atmosphere hadn't eased by much; most of the regulars were watching Nate's face, and the tension in Gavin's muscles suggested in unsubtle tones that he'd not always run a coffee-shop for a living.

Nate had considered options, and then shrugged and said, "Can I ask about the eighties music, then, because I've kinda been wondering?" In his peripheral vision, a table of what in retrospect were obviously selkies began collecting bets, possibly in regard to his reaction. Gavin had turned impressively pink and muttered something that sounded like, "I liked the eighties." A voice behind Nate's shoulder'd volunteered, to general merriment, "Yeah, just don't ask how long it took to get his fashion sense out of them," and the world had exhaled and gone on turning.

In the present, Nate turned his hand, laced their fingers together, held that gaze in his. Said, very softly, "I could use a break?" and received the answering curl of generous smile.

Gavin's studio apartment above the café was built of wood-beams and spaciousness and odd little metal-work sculptures in unexpected places: a copper bird tilting its head at them above the fireplace, a glittering bronze-lace horse captured mid-motion along one of the bookshelves, a playable miniature harp on the shelf beside the refrigerator. He tended to shrug when asked about them, and sometimes gave them away as presents. He never made weapons.

The largest bookshelf had the Arthur book someplace on it. Nate tended to hide it, these days less out of flattered embarrassment and more because he'd not yet run out of places with which to surprise blue eyes. He wasn't sure how he'd top leaving it carefully plastic-wrapped between layers of sponge cake in the refrigerator, but he was going to try.

They ran out of the narrow staircase and into the open space hand in hand; Gavin kicked the door shut with one definitive foot, and the rain danced over the windowpane. "I love you," Nate said, and tossed sketchbooks in the direction of the table; good timing, too, because a second later practiced warrior muscles knocked him off his feet and onto the couch, and then made sure he landed safely.

He inquired, raising eyebrows, "Did you do that last part in combat, too, or is it just me?" and Gavin sighed and balanced atop him, hips pressed into his and arousal evident but eyes very slightly wistful. "You could at least let me teach you to defend yourself with a knife...."

Nate, who knew exactly how much that offer meant coming from someone who'd sworn not to craft another weapon—object or person—slid fingers up to tangle in dark hair, feeling the glide of it like black silk over his own human fingers. "Maybe. Not today. Not in bed. Though if you ever felt like taking me captive...."

"Why would I," Gavin inquired, and leaned down to brush lips across Nate's throat, "when I already have you, mo chroi?"

"You know you could be calling me anything. Insults. Terrible nicknames. Baby animals." Nate wrapped a leg around his waist. Gavin was several inches shorter than he was, a fact which had never fully registered—ex-gods with charismatic calm smiles tended to fill up available space—until the first time they'd kissed. He secretly adored the disparity. Made it easier to tuck his boyfriend in under his arm in chilly weather. Something no one else ever properly got to see about Gavin. His. Theirs. "Also remind me to show you some things on the internet. Later. Do you still have boots on?"

"... no?"

"Not now, you mean."

"Sorry. You make me impatient. My heart. What I said. You are."

"Yeah," Nate said, "but what makes you think I trust you, the person who told me entirely seriously that flying pigs used to be real in Ireland?"

"I didn't think you'd believe me!" But they were both laughing, at that. Gavin sat up and managed to lose both the faded Whitesnake t-shirt and clinging black jeans in one sinuous movement. The tattoo rippled across his arm. Nate lay there appreciating the view, at least until blue eyes turned positively wicked and fingers made a gesture at the air.

"Oh, come on!"

"It's hardly fair that I'm the only one naked, now, is it?"

"Yeah," Nate sighed, not protesting his own abrupt nudity. Completely the desired eventual result, after all. "I lose more good shirts to you doing that, though."

"Oh. Sorry. They're not gone. Just... banished."

"You banished my clothes."

"I can get them back. Ah... probably. You wouldn't have a black walnut wand lying around, would you?"

"Right," Nate said, "just stop talking and kiss me," and tugged that head down to his.

If he'd known enough to wonder, the first time they'd kissed, he might've wondered what kissing a god would be like. He hadn't known, then; he wasn't sure he'd have expected reverence. Gavin kissed like sunrise on a winter morning: not tentative but in awe, every touch an exploration, every tiny lip-lick and nibble a shy explosion of light across previously untouched vistas. At the moment those kisses tasted of coffee and cinnamon and cream from Nate's own purloined mug; he had to laugh, and Gavin tapped fingers over his hip in not-actually-annoyed commentary and then followed the fingers with lips.

"Oh God—"

"Yes?"

"That's... not as funny as it was the first eighty times... oh—"

That mouth, hot and wet and deliciously skilled, closing over him; that tongue, licking and caressing and teasing, coaxing ready droplets out; finding rhythm and cadence and suction, oh dear God—

Gavin paused. Fingers found the base of Nate's arousal. Squeezed: not hard, but enough to hold off the tumble over the precipice. Nate, falling apart into need and sensation, swore at him, breathless and dizzy.

"I don't think that last one's anatomically possible even for a deity," Gavin mused, and went back to licking him. Nate, one leg sliding off the patchwork sofa, managed to lift his head enough to watch, to see himself disappearing into that glorious mouth; Gavin, sensing the gaze, looked up. And then smiled, and went back to doing what he'd been doing, only more slowly. Messily. Letting the length rest over sticky lips for a moment in between. Putting on a show.

"Please," Nate pleaded. Begged. Prayed. He was losing track. "Please."

"If you're asking nicely," Gavin murmured, and slid that mouth all the way down, fingers slipping lower to play with delicate intimate skin, tongue stroking just there—

Nate quite possibly screamed. He couldn't tell. Too much lightning through his veins.

After, collapsed boneless over the brightly hued sofa-pillows, he waved a worn-out hand. "You—I love you, you—wait, your turn—"

Gavin, sitting on the floor between Nate's spread thighs, actually blushed, and turned his head to press a kiss to the inside of the closest knee. A loose swoop of black hair swung forward to shadow the line of his jaw. "You don't have to."

"Oh no," Nate said, "come up here," and put both hands on broad shoulders and tugged. Under most circumstances this would be akin to tugging at a brick wall, but they'd long since established that supernatural strength couldn't withstand requests from this particular source. "I love you. And there is no way in this or any other realm that I'm not gonna touch you right now."

This earned a laugh, albeit with a hint of ancient-hillside ruefulness. "I do like you touching me."

"Well, then." He knew why, or thought he did. There were a lot of pieces of that why. One of them lay in the bright fascinated way blue eyes watched his hands while he drew: making art, creating stories out of nothing. One of them hid behind the faded silver-pink scar along that wrist. One of them simply had to do with being a once-god of hospitality and protection, and a consequent tendency to put every other person first. Nate on more than one occasion had locked the door that led down the stairs to the café, stood in front of it, and announced that they were taking a day off.

At the moment he'd successfully got his boyfriend off the floor and onto the couch, the melancholy lingered, just a hint, so he didn't push. Only touched a fingertip to that wondering smile— Gavin kissed it—and then trailed it over fair skin, the arch of a cheekbone, the quirk of an eyebrow. Gavin shut his eyes, head tipping into the caress; Nate leaned forward and kissed him. The angle was awkward and probably too clumsy, elbows and knees in wrong places. Didn't matter. Perfect.

Perfect, he thought again, and nudged at shoulders until they ended up sprawled out over the sofa with himself on top, legs tangled together, Gavin's body warm and compact and willing under his. He'd never been good at thinking that word. Perfect. Hell, he'd been nearly literally a starving artist until a few short years ago, tall and gawky and tentative with people, and he to this day wasn't quite used to having enough money to both pay rent and buy food. And he'd forever have the memory of the bruises from the day his father'd caught him kissing his first-ever high-school boyfriend on a sunny afternoon.

Gavin knew that story, of course. Gavin knew everything about him. Not from glancing through his mind. Because Nate had told him.

Now, he left the imprints of kisses across Gavin's flat stomach, honed ridges and planes of muscle. Traced shapes with leisurely fingers, crooked invisible hearts and spirals and knotwork decorating pale skin and battle scars. Gavin shivered but stayed quiet, eyes huge and blue-black as twilight oceans.

"My heart," he agreed, soft as the rain falling beyond the window, and kissed the crease between thigh and left hip; observed the resultant tiny gasp and squirm with satisfaction. "Can I watch you come, for me? Can I... make you come for me?"

"Please," Gavin whispered, eyelashes flickering down and up; an admission, a concession, sweetly and freely given, and any last hesitance dissolved in open desire. He did want that; they both wanted that. Very, very much.

"I love you," Nate told him one more time, and fit a hand between their bodies, finding the whole rigid length of him and closing fingers and palm around the heat. He knew the places Gavin liked to be touched, knew the exact degree of roughness and quickness that'd get the quick gasps and moans and shudders. Knew the reaction he'd get to the element of surprise, fingers rubbing over a straining tip without warning, without a pattern to the touches, no way to predict.

He was still lying more or less on top; he had the other hand in black hair, cradling it against the tattered knit exuberance of the pillows, and he leaned down for one more kiss, chasing the lingering taste of cinnamon cappuccino and indefinable elemental wildness; magic and kindness and pure rightness like coming home. When their lips met, he moved his hand just there. Gavin caught breath, arched up against him, and came, spilling across Nate's hand and their stomachs and bare skin.

The rain chose that moment to burst into noisy stormy applause.

Gavin started laughing. Nate buried his face in his boyfriend's neck and muttered, "When did you annoy a thunder god, and why...."

"Last Tuesday, when I told him we didn't serve alcohol." They didn't, not because Gavin was intrinsically opposed—no one who could drink that much whiskey could be—but because there were good reasons for not encouraging gods and water spirits and luck-dragons to become tipsy. One foot rubbed gently along Nate's calf. "Better?"

"Always." Always, always. The tensions of the day, the irritation of not being able to find an inspiration in pencil-dust and lines, ebbed and gave way to the all-encompassing afterglow. He'd come up with something. He knew he would. In the pages of folklore texts, or the iridescence of the storm clouds. In the flushed taste of Gavin's shoulder under his mouth.

On second thought, that last one was just for them. He mumbled, exhausted and content and needing to know, "You? Better?"

"As you said. Always." With arms around his back, holding him in place. Despite stickiness and sweat. And then, thoughtfully, "I used to have a cow."

Nate, at this point long used to the non-sequitur conversations—he'd come to the conclusion that maybe it was a god thing, but probably it was just his boyfriend—ventured patiently, "Was it a magical cow?"

"In fact yes. The Glas Glabhnenn. The Cow of Abundance. I'm not certain what happened to her; she got stolen at some point, by some heroes, and I lost track... the point was that her milk would fill any vessel you provided, and she had backwards hoofprints, to thwart potential reivers... would that be of use? As far as stories?"

"Huh." Maybe, maybe. A children's book, of course, but... a magical cow. Adventures with milk and cattle-thieves and Irish folk heroes. Comedy, but also adventure..."I've never drawn a cow. I could try it."

Gavin didn't say anything. Didn't need to. Only smiled, where Nate could feel it, lips pressed over his temple.

"I could put you in the story. As her owner."

"Please don't."

"You're beautiful."

"I'm not a hero."

"No," Nate said, and propped himself up on an elbow, put his chin in one hand, studied blue eyes. "You're something else."

They'd talked about the logistics, once, once so far. They'd had to, after the first clumsy declarations of love. A god, or someone who'd been for all practical purposes divine, and a human; Gavin'd said hesitantly, "I could—I used to, one of my duties for the family—it's been centuries since I've prepared it, but there's a feast of immortality...." Nate had swallowed hard, and thought about that.

He was still thinking. Whatever Gavin was these days—café owner, magical creature, Celtic legend—that list included immortal, or near to it; his own weapons would work, and a few remained, scattered around the world like poisonous leaves. He could choose to leave the human world and vanish into the faerie realm as so many of the others had, or even beyond to unmapped places. He hadn't so far. Because, he'd said, our people need someplace to go while they're here.

Immortality for Nate would mean watching human friends and acquaintances and the world he'd known and even the family who'd disowned him crumble under the weight of time. He'd never age, he'd asked about that, but that would mean he'd *never age*.

He knew Gavin didn't expect him to say yes.

He knew Gavin had never offered as much for anyone else. Not ever, not in all those terrible empty centuries.

He lay there with his legs tangled up in Gavin's, listening to the carefree drumsong of the storm. They were breathing in unison. He could feel it.

He drew a curving loop, with a fingertip, over Gavin's collarbone. A sideways figure-eight. Infinity. Drawing forever. Art, forever. Magical cows and coffee that would never grow cold. Kisses under sunshine, kisses flavored with mocha and enchantment, kisses in the rain.

"If I can't put you in the story," he said, "can I move in with you?" and Gavin went absolutely immobile under him, eyes wide.

"Can you—yes, yes, *ar ndóigh*, of course—but why—oh, no, did something happen to your apartment, do you need someplace to stay, why didn't you tell me sooner—"

"No," Nate said, hoping he didn't sound as desperate as he

thought he might, "no, nothing, I just—I don't need a place to stay. I want to. If you want. Um. I mean sort of not temporary. More sort of... forever."

"Oh," Gavin said, near-soundlessly, but those eyes were shining with the beginnings of delight, like the beginnings of everything, like hope, "still yes, then. Of course. Forever."

Magic Beans
Django Wexler

The alley behind Apollo's wasn't the kind of place I enjoyed hanging out at any hour, much less four in the morning. In daylight, it was cramped and unpleasant, stinking of whatever trash was baking in the steel dumpsters that lined it on both sides. By night it was equally fragrant, but with 100% more impenetrable shadows, perfect for hiding unnamable terrors of the darkness or murderous hobos. All told, I would much rather have been snug in my bed in the semi-furnished attic of John's Comics and Collectibles ($450 / month, utilities included, must be willing to tolerate raucous D&D until the small hours of the morning) than standing out here waiting to be knifed and/or consumed by ravenous beasts from beyond the stars.

Needs must, though, when the devil drives. With "the devil" in this case being "my penis." Or possibly "Daniella Atherton." Or possibly a conspiracy between the two. It would take two such evil geniuses to so thoroughly ruin a good night's sleep, just when I needed every bit of strength to energetically fail my Linear Algebra exam tomorrow afternoon.

I slammed on the sliding back steel door again with my free hand, and heard the snick of the lock from inside. The door rattled open half an inch, giving me a view of a bright green eye.

"Who is it?" Danny said.

"Who do you think it is?" I said. "How many people do you get banging on the back door at four in the morning?"

"Wouldn't you like to know."

"Would you let me in?"

"Did you bring my curry?"

I held up a package wrapped in green paper. "Yes, I brought your curry. Now open the door, the rats are massing for an attack."

"No rats out there," Danny said, pulling the door the rest of the way open in a chorus of squeaks and groans. "They were all eaten by the giant spiders."

"Oh, lovely."

I stepped past her, and she hauled the door shut again, grunting with the effort. Once she'd locked and bolted it, she turned back to me, and I leaned in for a kiss.

I had to lean quite far. Danny brushes five feet tall only in thick-soled shoes, though she can add an inch or two if she teases her blue-and-purple hair into spikes. She's as pale as things that live under rocks and fear the light of day, and stick thin in spite of an enthusiastically unhealthy diet and a voracious, unpredictable appetite. One of the perils of dating her is the occasional frantic four AM text demanding curry.

"Thank god," she said, pulling away from me and grabbing for the green paper package. "I was literally going to die if I didn't get something to eat before the end of my shift."

"Literally?" I said.

"Literally. They'd find me in the morning, shriveled into a desiccated corpse. 'Local Barista Wastes Away During Overnight Shift, Film at 11.'"

"There's always the scones at the counter."

"Have you ever tried one of those things?"

"No."

"Neither has anyone else. Ever. I don't think you could break one open with a chisel."

She carried the curry through the back of Apollo's. (The name has to be a joke, but I've never been able to find anyone to admit to it.) Since Danny and I started dating, I'd become intimately familiar with the rear of the coffee shop, places that normal men were not meant to wot of. There was the storeroom, where the back door opened onto the alley and bulk supplies were kept; the kitchen, almost entirely occupied by coffee-making apparatus; a tiny employee bathroom; and the sex closet.

The kitchen had a tiny table, on which Danny deposited the

curry before busying herself with one of the machines. Coffee machines always looked vaguely alien to me, all plastic and chrome with mysterious spigots and levers, inexplicably hot or cold to the touch and prone to making unexpected glooping noises. The one Danny was fiddling with was even stranger than most, a blocky monster of a thing whose plexiglass front offered a glimpse into a complicated network of grinders, bubblers, boilers, and other arcane apparatus. A maw at the top gaped ominously; Danny tore the top off a small container and dumped a rattling handful of beans inside, standing on tiptoe.

"Is this new?"

"Uh-huh. The very latest. It's for special magic beans."

"Magic beans," I dead-panned.

She handed me one of the small, round containers off a stack beside the machine. It said 'MAGIC BEANS' on the label, with a picture of a startled Jack staring up at an enormous beanstalk.

"I don't think Jack planted coffee beans," I said, handing it back. "I mean, they wouldn't grow after you roasted them."

"Pedant. They installed it this evening and I haven't gotten a chance to try it yet." Danny threw a big Frankenstein-style switch, and the machine startled to rumble. "It's alive!"

I watched the thing for a moment as rollers rolled, grinder ground, and bubblers started to bubble. "How long does it take?"

"A while." Danny sighed. "We need to talk, but not until after I've had coffee and something to eat."

"All right." The devil was getting hopeful signals here, and practically jumped for joy when Danny's eyes flicked to the sex closet. I raised my eyebrows, and she pushed herself back from the counter and unlocked the door with a key from the ring on her belt. The kitten calendar hanging from the front of the door flapped as she pulled it open.

"It's weird to have a kitten calendar on the door of the sex closet," I told her, stepping inside.

"Would you stop calling it the sex closet?" she said. "I have to come in here like fifty times a day for beans and shit. Calling it the sex closet makes that weird."

The sex closet is fairly roomy, and lined with a few shelves at head height piled with replacement alien-coffee-machine parts and filters. The floor is piled high with plastic sacks of coffee beans, which are just about stable and soft enough to be useful. When Danny pulled the door closed behind us, she left us in complete, coffee-scented darkness. By the time I'm old, I'm going to have a weird fetish for the smell of coffee beans, and I'm going to send Danny the therapy bills.

"I mean, we do use it for sex," I said. There was a rustle as she pulled off her apron and tossed it aside.

"We had sex in your car," Danny said, coming closer. She put her hands on my chest and pushed me gently backward until I came up against the mound of sacks. "Does that make it 'the sex car?' Would you be comfortable visiting your mother in the sex car?"

I had a witty rejoinder to that, I swear, but about that moment her mouth found mine and I decided not to bother. I leaned in to the kiss, slipping my hands down her flanks to her ass and then up the small of her back, untucking her shirt as I went. She gave a little gasp and pressed herself tighter against me, my leg tangling between hers. Her hands were on my back, nails scratching lightly over my skin, sliding up under my shirt to my shoulders.

Then, in one smooth motion, she pulled herself up and wrapped her legs tight around my waist. I staggered a bit under the weight— she's thin, but not that thin—and spun her around until I could rest her on the bags of coffee, without letting my lips come off of hers. Not an easy maneuver, but I'd had practice. She clung tight at the waist, the top button of her jeans digging in to my chest, but leaned back enough that I could worm my hands between us and undo the buttons of her store-issue flannel shirt. Nothing under it but smooth skin. It hung from her shoulders, brushing against my ear as I kissed a gentle line down the side of her throat, lingering on her collarbone, and then down to the slight swell of her breast.

We stayed that way for a while, her hands under my shirt while I kissed her all over, sliding my fingers over her flanks and pinching her nipples to hear the hitch in her breath. Her hips moved against my stomach, rocking gently, until all of a sudden she was moving me away and fumbling at the buttons on her jeans. It took her a moment to kick her shoes off and wriggle out of them, and I took the opportunity to get naked. She grabbed hold of my hand and pulled me closer so she could wrap her legs around me again.

From the moment I pushed into her, I could tell something was different. Something practically crackled between us, a weird kind of energy I'd never felt before, running over her bare skin like static wherever I touched her, arcing when our lips touched. I felt charged with it, every bit of me thrumming and wild, and from the way she moved I could tell she felt it too. I curled my fingers in her pixie-short hair, and if there had been any light I was sure I'd have seen every strand standing on end.

Danny doesn't make noise during sex. It's very convenient for when we're using the sex closet, but I mean she never makes noise; I've felt her have hip-shaking, toe-curling, sheet-clenching orgasms without much more than a little gasping. This time, as she pulled herself tight against me, there was a sound. Not a moan, just the slightest little 'ah' at the back of her throat, but it was the most erotic thing I'd ever heard. We finished together moments later, her hips bucking to the soft crunch of coffee beans as my fingers tightened on her shoulders and I let out a long, raspy breath.

It was the best sex we'd ever had, bar none. That strange energy flowed through us as we came together, and left me with a feeling of peace and lassitude even more profound than the usual post-coital bliss. I would have been happy to stand there forever, Danny's arms and legs wrapped around me, and just listen to her breathe.

"Holy shit," Danny said, after a few moments of respectful silence.

"Yeah," I breathed.

"I need curry."

"Is this really the time for curry?"

"This is exactly the time for curry."

"I think this thing is broken," I said, when she emerged from the bathroom a minute later. "Nothing's coming out."

"That's what she said," Danny said, automatically.

I tapped the alien coffee device, patiently. The pot at the bottom was indeed completely devoid of coffee, though a thick mist was seeping from the little spigot, as though it were full of dry ice. Danny came over and peer at it, then stood on tiptoes again to look into the input chamber.

"Huh," she said. "The beans are gone."

"Are they supposed to be gone?"

"How should I know? It didn't come with a manual." She looked around and shrugged. "Fuck it. I can call them in the morning."

She poured herself a cup of coffee from a batch produced by one of the more mundane devices, and opened the green paper package. Steam and the smell of spicy food wafted out of it. I stood in silence for a moment as she shoveled rice and curry hot enough to set off radiation alarms into her mouth.

"So what did you want to talk about?"

"Mmf," Danny said, taking a gulp of coffee. "Right. I wanted to tell you that I think you and I, as a couple, are not going to work."

"Okay," I said, and then as my brain caught up to my ears, "wait, what?"

"You know. It's fun and all, but no."

"Are you serious?" A look at her face told me she was. "You're breaking up with me."

"Mmmhmm," she said, swallowing another forkful.

"Am I allowed to ask why?"

Mouth full, she merely raised an eyebrow.

"Is it about that thing from the other day? It is, isn't it?"

Danny, while drinking her coffee, made a gesture with her free hand that implied it might or might not be.

"Look, if it's that important to you, I'll say it. I lov—"

"Doesn't work if I have to extort it out of you," Danny said. "Come on, Brian. I asked what you thought, and you gave me an honest answer."

"But...." My brain was still a little fogged. "But what about what just happened?"

"What just happened?"

"You know. The best sex we ever had?"

"It really was," Danny said thoughtfully. "Nice to finish on a high note, so to speak."

"Why didn't you tell me this before?"

Danny, mouth full again, raised an eyebrow that indicated the answer to that question should be self-evident.

"Dragging me into the sex closet when you're planning on breaking up with me seems pretty questionable, ethically speaking," I said.

"First," she said, swallowing the last of the coffee, "don't pout, it looks terrible on you. Second, don't call it a sex closet. And third, if I'd said, 'Hey, we're breaking up, but do you want to have sex one more time?' don't pretend that you wouldn't have said yes."

"I would have thought about it," I said. "Hard."

"Of course you would have." She wadded the paper around the curry container and shot it expertly into the trash. "Now, if you'll excuse me, I have to get back to the counter. Half an hour is usually about the limit of Lisa's patience."

Strictly speaking, I ought to have gone home at that point, but I was suffering from a severe conflict of stimuli and needed someone to talk to. There's always someone in Apollo's, even at four in the morning. It's the only twenty-four-hour coffeeshop in town, and we are a famously hard-drinking university when it comes to caffeinated beverages.

I slipped out through the swinging doors to emerge behind the counter. Apollo's was a large place, booths lining both walls, big windows at the front of the shop with a scattering of tables, chairs, and freestanding displays in between. The counter was crowded—there was a university tradition of putting fund-raising boxes for various causes there, each accompanied by a plush animal with a sign pleading for donations. As I skirted the edge, I bumped a smiling dolphin raising money for the swim team's trip to Jamaica; it fell over and rolled belly-up on the floor, staring up at me with accusing eyes, and I kicked it viciously out of the way. The confusion in my gut was rapidly rotting into fetid anger.

"Brian!" Evan Ngyuen, my freshman roommate and sometime best friend, waved to me from a table in the corner. I slouched in his direction, wishing there were more dolphins to kick. On the way, I nearly ran into his sister Lisa, who dodged adroitly and headed back toward the counter with a tray tucked under her arm. Lisa doesn't actually work at Apollo's, but she sometimes gets drafted in to cover Danny's breaks.

"Hey, Bri," Evan said, a nickname which I hate. He punched me playfully on the arm, which I also hate. I slumped into the chair opposite him and waited for him to notice my hangdog expression, which he resolutely refused to do. "How are we feeling about this Linear Algebra exam? I'm feeling great. I'm loose, I'm excited, I am so ready to fail. I am going to fail so hard. People are going to hear me failing on the other side of the quad."

"What are you doing here, then?"

"Putting on the finishing touches," Evan said. "A sleepless night before failing an exam adds a certain je ne sais quoi, you know?" He leaned back, grinning. "What about you?"

"I've been better," I said.

"Oh no." Evan leaned forward. "You're not going to pass, are you?"

"No. Not a chance."

"Okay. You had me worried for a minute there. We can't have you wrecking the curve, sir."

I got tired of waiting for him to ask what was wrong. "Danny broke up with me."

"Wait, what?"

"That's exactly what I said."

"When was this?" Evan said.

"Just now. Literally sixty seconds ago. In the kitchen."

"Why? I mean, in some sense, I know why. She's always been so far out of your league that you weren't even playing the same sport, but she seemed relatively happy with the situation, for reasons I personally have never been able to—"

"Evan," I grated, "I am really not in the mood."

"Sorry." He had the grace to look contrite. 'Paying attention to what other humans are feeling' is a strange and foreign country for Evan. "But did she tell you why?"

I looked over my shoulder at the counter. Danny had emerged, and was talking quietly to Lisa. Aside from Evan and me, there were three other customers in the shop. Gil and Jason, a couple I knew, were in a booth together, bent so far over their books that they were nearly bumping foreheads. A pretty blonde girl I'd never seen before sat by the door, listening to headphones and reading a paperback. None of them were close enough to overhear. The big front windows showed only darkness and a mirrored version of the coffeeshop.

"We had a fight," I said. "About a week ago."

"Did you do something stupid?"

"No!" I said. "At least, I didn't think so at the time. She started asking me strange questions."

"Strange like, 'What's the capital of Algeria multiplied by orange?', or strange like, 'What kind of sheets would you use, hypothetically speaking, if you wanted to slit someone's throat without leaving any DNA evidence?'"

"Like about what I was going to do after graduation."

"Oh," Evan said. "You mean strange."

"Right? Like I can think that far ahead."

"I have a firm policy of only thinking about things up to three days in the future," Evan said. "Anything after that can be ignored."

I actually believe he lived that way. It would explain his grades. "I told her I didn't know."

"Guys," said Lisa, from over by the front door.

"And she dumped you a week later?"

"There was some other stuff." I shifted uncomfortably. Talking about capital L Love or its lack with Evan seemed like a bad idea. "I don't know. Maybe...."

He waited patiently for me to finish the sentence.

"Guys?" Lisa said. "There's a dragon."

"I mean, should I have lied to her?" I said. "Is that what she wanted?"

"Who knows?" Evan said. "I mean, girls, right?"

"Guys," Lisa shouted, a touch of hysteria entering her voice. "There is a fucking dragon right fucking outside the door!"

At that point, quite a few things happened at once:

I shot to my feet.

Danny said, "Holy shit!" and dropped the mug she was carrying.

Evan twisted in his seat, then scrambled up and onto the table, butt-first, knocking over his empty cup.

Jason, facing the door, attempted to shoot to his feet, but his ample stomach shoved the table forward into Gil.

Gil tried to look around, took the corner of the table straight to the solar plexus, and folded up, gasping.

The blonde by the door turned a page in her book, oblivious.

The dragon put both front paws on one of the windows, like a puppy on display in a pet store. It was about the size of a pony, covered in slab-like red and black scales that slid over one another as it moved in a ballet of interlocking armor. A pair of bat-like wings lay neatly folded against its sides. Its head, mounted on a long, flexible neck, featured two glowing red eyes and a dog-like snout, as well as a mouth full of triangular shark teeth and a thin, forked tongue sliding between them. Its paws had talons several inches long, which it was using to scratch long sets of parallel lines in the glass.

"What the fuck?" Evan said.

"It's trying to get in!" Lisa said, backing rapidly against the counter.

"Okay," Danny said, with trademark pragmatism. "It can't get in. The glass is practically bulletproof. Everyone get away from the window—"

Jason had extricated himself from the table and was helping his fallen boyfriend. The dragon slammed one paw against the glass, but Danny seemed to be correct—the thick plastic-y sheet bowed, but held. Just beyond it, the blonde girl read on. I wondered what book was that absorbing.

The dragon drew in a deep breath, reared back, and breathed fire at the window. A stream of white-hot flame broke against the glass, which immediately spider-webbed with cracks. Lisa screamed, which made the blonde girl look up, at last, but in the wrong direction.

"Shit," I said.

I was already running, dodging the tables and fallen chairs. The dragon crouched like a cat and sprang at the window, its full weight punching through the glass like rotten cardboard. The girl turned around and froze, eyes going very wide, as the dragon's front paws landed on her table. It took a step forward, shivering its wings to shake off the remains of the window, and she scrambled away. Cat-like again, the thing pounced, catching her in the back with one paw and slamming her to the ground. She rolled over to find it staring down at her from only inches away, fanged mouth open wide.

"Hey!" I shouted, hurling one of the flimsy plastic chairs. It bounced off the dragon's armored flank, and the creature's head snapped around. "That's right, over here!"

The dragon stepped forward, across the girl's trembling form and in my direction. I retreated, looking over my shoulder to make sure there was no one behind me. The monster's expression didn't seem cruel, aside from the razor-sharp teeth. There was a feeling of curiosity there. Also, one of its back legs didn't seem to be moving properly, and now that it was closer I could see something black sticking out from between the scales of its thigh.

I stepped back next to a display cabinet, which was piled high with two-pound bags of the house blend. Keeping my movements slow and careful, I picked one up, hefted it, and then threw it as hard as I could over the dragon's shoulder. I'd hoped it would work like throwing a toy to a dog, but I'd underestimated the dragon's speed. Its head snapped out, snagging the bag out of the air. Beans sprayed everywhere as it chewed and swallowed, belching out a brief spurt of flame.

"O... kay," I said aloud. "Any helpful suggestions?"

"Fucking run!" said Evan.

"If I run it'll jump on me," I said. The dragon matched my slow movements with its own unhurried stride, but it was clearly ready to pounce. "And then that girl will get eaten."

"I've got a knife!" Lisa produced a Swiss army knife with a three-inch blade, which she attempted to fold into the proper configuration with shaking hands.

"I doubt that's going to help," I said, with what I thought was remarkable aplomb. "But thank you."

"Throw it more coffee!" said Danny.

"I think—" I said.

"Look at it! It's getting woozy!"

I turned my attention back to the dragon and saw that she was right. Its steps had become uncertain, and the way its head weaved suggested the movements of a drunk. It wasn't a great plan, but it was the best in a field of one, so I grabbed another bag of coffee and threw it right at the dragon's head.

As before, it caught the bag and chomped it down. This time the effect was obvious. The dragon wobbled on its feet, peering blearily in all directions. I underhanded it the next bag of beans, and it nearly missed the catch, tearing the bag in half and sending beans rattling across the floor. After gulping down what was left, it sat back heavily on its haunches, then rolled painfully onto one side, tucked in its head, and promptly went to sleep.

"Holy fucking shit," Evan said, articulating what seemed to be the general sentiment. He stepped forward, hesitantly, from where he had heroically been trying to hide behind Danny. "You totally slayed a dragon!"

"Slain," Lisa said, coming closer.

"Slew," said Jason, in his breathy, quiet voice. "He slew a dragon. Or has slain one."

"But he hasn't," Gil said, rubbing his stomach. "Because it's not dead. Look, it's still breathing."

"It must metabolize coffee differently than we do," Jason said.

Gil and Jason are something of an odd couple. Gil is a junior in theatre, and cuts a Byronic figure with high cheekbones and emaciated good looks. He wears a post-post-ironic goatee, reads poetry in public, and listens to bands you've never heard of, but in spite of all that he manages to be a genuinely likable human being. Gil and Danny have been friends since they were toddlers, and were in a (very) short-lived band together.

Jason, while also friendly when you get to know him, is more the retiring type. Before he and Gil started dating, it was rare to see him outside a kind of groove he'd worn between his room and the cafeteria. He's large and heavily bearded in a way that screams "future sysadmin," and in a more perfect world he would be training to be something totally other, like a world-class concert pianist. But because stereotypes sometimes just work out, he is both a junior in computer science and a level 95 Night Elf Druid.

"Can we leave the grammar debate to one side," Danny said, "and talk about why there is a dragon in my coffee shop?"

"Are you okay?" I said to the girl I didn't know, working my around the sleeping bulk of the dragon.

She blinked, looking up at me and adjusting her glasses. "I don't think so."

"Are you hurt?" I bent over to help her up. "I think Danny has a first aid kit."

"No, I mean, I'm not hurt, but I think I've gone crazy." She grabbed my wrist and hauled herself up. "I could have sworn that was a dragon about to eat me."

"You're not crazy," I said, gesturing to the rest of the group, which had gathered around the dozing dragon. "Or at least, if you are, we're all crazy too."

"Damn," she said. "Any other explanation is going to be a hell of a lot more trouble."

"What's your name?"

"Anna."

"I'm Brian." I kept hold of her hand, which was soft and warm. "Let me introduce you to the others."

"It could be CGI," Evan was saying as we came over. "I mean, it's possible. They can do crazy things with computers these days. Did you see Avatar?"

"That's not right," Danny said. "That's not even wrong. You can't—you know what, never mind. What do those of you with more than two brain cells think?"

There was a long moment of silence, during which Anna and I joined the circle. Danny raised an eyebrow.

"Sorry," Gil said. "We weren't sure who you were referring to."

"Everyone but Evan," Danny said. "And Brian, but I'm awarding him an honorary third brain cell for bravery."

"Aw, harsh," said Evan.

"It looks like a pretty standard dragon," Jason said. "Hexapodal, which I always thought was weird. Scales. Breathes fire. Straightforward."

"Where the hell did it come from?" Danny said.

"Danny," Lisa said, moving over to the hole the dragon had left in the front window, "can you turn on the outside lights?"

Danny gave her a quizzical look, but went over to a panel behind the counter and flipped a couple of switches. A couple of big bulbs flickered to life under the awning, over the area that was used for patio seating in better weather. There was a collective gasp from the room as they pushed back the darkness.

The patio was gone. The street was gone, and so was the laundromat-slash-porno-video-rental shop across the way. In their place was a jagged landscape of dark rocks, obsidian spikes poking up through gray-green bedrock like spears.

"Oh," said Jason, not betraying much surprise. "So the question isn't where the dragon came from, it's where have we gone."

"What?" Gil said. "We haven't gone anywhere. We're here in Apollo's."

"Which has apparently been transported to the top of Mount Doom." Lisa opened the front door, making the bell jingle and eliciting another mutual gasp.

"Lisa!" Evan said. "Careful."

"It's just rocks." Lisa poked them with her foot, then stepped outside. "Seems normal enough. Except for not being normal at all."

"What the fuck?" said Evan. When that failed to produce any answers, he said it again. "What the fuck?"

"Thank you for that," Danny said. "Okay, I take it nobody has any idea how this happened? Nobody ran over any old gypsy women—"

"Roma," Lisa said, "you should say Roma, and—"

"—Roma women, thank you for that, or made any deals with the devil or saw a flying saucer or anything like that?"

Gil and Jason shook their heads. Evan shrugged. I said, "Nothing magic here. Unless you count—"

My eyes locked on Danny's, and we finished together. "—the magic beans!"

A few moments later, all seven of us were crowded uncomfortably into a kitchen meant for three at most. Danny had a small clear space in front of the new coffee monstrosity, where she was examining one of the canisters of beans.

"They delivered them with the machine," she said. "There was a note saying we were getting this as a free trial, or something."

There were six of the little cans left. Danny shook one, and shrugged.

"Sounds like coffee beans to me." She tore it open and sniffed. "Smells like them, too."

"Okay," Gil said. "So maybe it's the machine that's magic."

"A magic coffee machine that transported the shop to another planet?" Evan said.

"Do you have any better ideas?" Jason said.

"One way to find out." Danny dumped the container of beans into the hopper and threw the big switch. The machine churned and gurgled into motion, bubbling and whirring. "Someone go check if anything changed."

Lisa darted out of the room. "Nope!" her voice came back, a moment later. "Still Mount Doom."

"It might take a while," I offered. "Maybe it only happens when the coffee is ready. Not that it produced any last time."

There was general muttering to the effect that this made sense, as much as anything made sense anymore. We drifted back into the front room, leaving Danny to watch the progress of the magic coffeemaker. I went back over to the sleeping dragon, and found Anna standing beside it.

"There's something stuck in its leg," she said. "See that black thing? It looks like the hilt of a sword."

She was right. I'd noticed the dragon had a bit of a limp.

"Think I should pull it out?" I said.

"It could be one of those thorn-from-a-lion's-paw things," she said.

"Or it could wake up and try to kill us again."

"Tell you what," she said. "You pull it out, and I'll be ready with another bag of coffee."

"Okay."

I watched the dragon for a while, but it gave no sign of moving.

The hilt of the sword fit neatly into my hand, and I gave it a tug, expecting resistance. To my surprise, the blade slid free as neatly as if I were drawing it from a scabbard. I pulled it all the way out, and black blood bubbled briefly in the wound, then scabbed over like cooling lava.

The dragon's head came up, and it blinked at me, blearily. I backed away. "Anna?"

"Here you go!" she said, off to one side. "Here, boy!"

The dragon turned, and at the sight of her hefting another bag of coffee rolled ponderously back onto its feet, eyes locked on the sack of beans. It was for all the world like a dog watching someone holding a slice of bacon.

"You... uh... should probably throw that," I said, as the dragon took a step closer.

Anna mimed throwing it toward the door, and the dragon's head followed the gesture before snapping back to her. She did it again, and again.

"Okay!" she said. "You ready? Go get it!"

She threw the bag, which sailed out the door with the dragon in hot pursuit. The coffee hit the hard ground and bounced, and the dragon was on it a few moments later, giving the bag a shake and then swallowing it whole. It snorted, blowing out a brief gout of flame, and then wandered off somewhat tipsily into the rocks.

"That worked better than I expected," Anna said.

"Yeah." I looked down at the sword. "So what do you think, magic sword?"

"Magic sword," she agreed.

It looked like a magic sword, long and elegant, with a single fuller running nearly the full length of the blade. Sparkles of blue-white light cascaded along its length whenever I moved it, making a crackling noise down at the edge of hearing.

I sighted carefully and swung it down at a nearby chair. The blade passed through it with no resistance at all, and the two halves fell away with a clatter.

"Right," I said. "Let's be very careful with this."

From the kitchen came a sigh of frustration. I set the sword on a table, gently, and went to see what was the matter.

"It's not working," Danny said, when we'd all gathered again. "Look, it's making coffee."

The pot under the magic coffeemaker was indeed filling up as a stream of brown liquid drooled from the spout.

"Isn't that what it's supposed to do?" Gil said.

"It didn't make any the first time," Danny said. "When it brought us to... wherever we are. Nothing came out but a little bit of smoke."

"Is there a dial or something?" Evan said. "Like on the side. A switch that says 'Make Coffee/Time Machine'?"

"It's not a time machine," Lisa said. "Because there wouldn't be dragons if we went back in time."

"I found a magic sword," I said, to no one in particular. When that failed to produce any praise, I added, "And Anna got rid of the dragon."

"I kind of liked the dragon," Gil said. "I was going to name him Carl."

"If we can focus for a moment," Danny said, "I would like to figure out a way off of Mount Doom. Which means getting this thing to work properly and not just make coffee."

"Have you tried kicking it?" Evan said.

Danny rolled her eyes. Jason cleared his throat.

"When you turned it on the first time, did you do anything else? Chant any spells or anything?"

"You said 'It's alive!'," I said. "And then..." I paused.

"And then what?" said Lisa.

"Maybe it's curry that was magic?" I said. "Magic curry. I mean, it could happen. Makes as much sense as magic beans."

"Don't change the subject," Lisa said. "What happened—"

"We had sex," Danny said, irritably.

"What?" Evan said. "Here on the table?"

"No," I said, "in the sex closet."

"Apollo's has a sex closet?" Gil said. "How did I not know this?"

"It's not a sex closet!" Danny said.

"More of a sex alcove, then, or—" Gil persisted.

"It's just a closet," Danny grated. "That one over there. With the kitten calendar."

"So you had sex," Lisa said. "While the coffee was brewing."

"And it transported us to another planet," Evan said.

"More like another universe," Lisa said, "because of all the magic."

"Not to mention that the electricity still works," Anna said. "Does anyone else think that's weird?"

We all agreed that it was very weird.

"Oh!" Lisa said. "I just thought of something. I'll be right back."

She rushed out of the kitchen. The six of us looked at one another, except for Anna, who looked down at her shoes.

"It seems obvious to me," Evan said. "Danny and Bri just have to get back into the sex closet and do the nasty while we brew another load. That should kick the magic coffeemaker into gear."

"No," Danny said.

"What do you mean, no?" Evan said. "This could be our only way to get home!"

"First of all, that's the most ridiculous thing I've ever heard—"

Gil coughed. "I have to admit, Danny, that once you've accepted a magic coffeemaker that transports you to other worlds, having it be powered by a sex closet isn't that much more of a stretch."

"—and second," Danny went on through gritted teeth, "Brian and I are officially broken up. So I will not be getting back in the closet with him. And it is not a sex closet."

"Broken up?" Gil said. "When did this happen?"

"This evening. Morning. Whatever," I said.

"We can talk about it later," Danny said.

Lisa came back into the kitchen, carrying her iPad. "The internet still works! I am totally live-tweeting this from here on out, you've all been warned."

"Too bad you didn't get a picture of the dragon," Gil said.

"Yeah!" Lisa looked around. "Did I miss anything?"

"It looks like the magic coffeemaker is sex-powered," Gil said.

"Really?"

"No," Danny said. "Not really. Because that is absurd."

"It's worth a try," Evan said.

"Does it have to be Danny and Brian?" Jason said. "If it's just feeding on the sexual... energy, or whatever, then maybe it can be anyone."

"I volunteer," Evan said immediately, "in the name of Science."

He raised his eyebrow in Danny's direction, and she rolled her eyes again and crossed her arms.

"Well," Gil said, after a moment of awkward silence. "Given that Jason and I appear to be the only official couple at this happy gathering, I suppose the experiment falls to us."

"I'm against it," Evan said. "What if gay sex makes it explode or something?"

"Then it has that in common with the brains of some of my relatives," Gil said. "But I still think it's worth a shot."

"Is it finished brewing?" I said.

Danny looked the machine over and nodded. "Looks like. The switch flips back up when it's done."

"In that case," Gil said, "open up another can of beans." He took Jason's hand, and Jason blushed under his beard. "And we will do our best."

After Gil and Jason were shut in the sex closet and the machine was brewing again, the rest of us retreated to the front room. I showed Lisa, Danny, and Evan the magic sword; Lisa was excited to take pictures for her Twitter, while Danny grumbled that I shouldn't have gone around slicing up perfectly good furniture. After that we sat around for a while, in silence.

A thump came from the direction of the kitchen and the closet, and a grunt.

"Oooookay," Evan said, shifting awkwardly. "So. How about that local sporting squadron?"

Anna looked at him quizzically, and Lisa and Danny just ignored him. I gave a weak chuckle, but couldn't come up with a follow-on.

"All right," Evan said. "So Danny, why did you break up with Brian?"

"Excuse me," I said, "is that really a subject we ought to be going over in public?"

"I'm just making conversation, man."

"Make it about something else!"

"I broke up with Brian," Danny said, "because he doesn't know how to think more than three months into the future."

"Come on," I said, "that's unfair. Just because I don't know what I'm going to do after graduation—"

"I don't intend to argue about it," Danny said.

"But I still don't understand what—"

She got up and walked back toward the counter. Evan gave me a look that said, 'Girls, eh?' Lisa frowned at something on her iPad.

Anna, by the door, said, "Hey! I think something's happening!"

We all looked around. Mount Doom was disappearing, fading away into a kind of gray-green static, like a broken TV seen through colored glass. The four of us stared, fascinated, as the static grew and peaked in total silence, then gradually faded away again. It left behind a wall of swirling white mist, so thick the overhead lights only penetrated a few feet.

After a few moments passed and nothing further occurred, I said, "Whatever was going to happen, I think that was it."

"Did it work?" Danny said, from the kitchen. "The coffeemaker didn't produce any coffee."

"I think so," Lisa called back. "Now we've got mist instead of black rocks."

"That sounds like a real improvement," Danny said, emerging from behind the counter.

I had to admit, as brave new worlds went, I'd seen more interesting ones. Tendrils of mist were coming in through the open door and the broken window, tentatively probing the tables and chairs. As hard as I stared, no solid shapes resolved through the silvery curtain of fog.

"Well," Danny said, after watching the hypnotic swirling for a while. "Now what?"

"Wherever this is, it isn't home," Evan said.

"Unless it just relocated us somewhere really foggy," Lisa said. "We could be in Florida or something."

"I've been to Florida," I said, "and I've never seen anything like this."

"So it's the Planet of Mists instead of the Planet of Dragons," Danny said. "Doesn't matter. What do we do now?"

"Try again?" Evan said. "There's plenty of beans left."

"I think Gil and Jason may need a bit of a rest," Anna said.

"I think we should go out and look around," Lisa said. "Florida's a big place. We'd feel really stupid if we turned out to be half a mile from an I-95 rest stop."

"I think I speak for everyone when I say there's no way in hell I'm going out there," Evan said.

"You don't speak for me," Lisa said. "I'll go. Even if this is some alien planet, I'd like to actually see it before we leave."

"Come on," Evan said. "You have no idea what's out there! It could be more dragons, or... something awful."

"I'll take a bag of coffee. That's all Brian had."

"Brian's a brave idiot," Evan said.

"Thank you," I muttered.

"And you're not going outside," he continued. "That's final."

"You don't get to tell me what to do," Lisa said.

"You're my sister," Evan snapped. "Mom and Dad—"

"Lisa's right," Danny interrupted. "We ought to have a look around."

"That doesn't mean it has to be her!" Evan said.

"Are you volunteering?"

Evan looked to me for support. I looked at Danny, then shrugged.

"She shouldn't go alone, anyway," Evan said. "Maybe Brian—"

"I'll go with her," Danny said.

"Wait," I said. "Hang on. Maybe I should go. What if you run into something nasty?"

"What makes you think you would be more helpful?" Danny said. "Besides, I'll take the magic sword."

She lifted the blade from where I'd left it on a table. It crackled faintly.

"Be careful with that," I said weakly. "You could cut your own arm off."

"Awesome," Lisa said. "Can I have a try with it?"

"We'll see."

Danny swung the blade, carefully, and took a deep breath. She met my eyes, and for a moment her mask cracked. She was scared, though she wouldn't have admitted it under torture. My heart lurched.

"I'll go," I said. "I mean, three will be better than two, right?"

"No," Danny said. "You guys stay here and mind the shop. We won't go far."

"What if you don't come back?" Evan said.

Danny gave him a withering look. "Then I guess you'll have to come and rescue us."

Gil and Jason emerged from the kitchen a few minutes after we watched Danny and Lisa vanish among the swirling clouds. I sat with Anna by the door, a bag of coffee in my lap, feeling thoroughly ridiculous. Evan was in a booth by himself, muttering darkly.

"What happened?" Gil said. "Did it work?"

"We think so," Anna said. "We've got mist, now. Lisa and Danny went out to see if they could find anything."

"By themselves?" Gil said.

"She took the magic sword," I said, a bit defensively.

He frowned. "You still ought to have gone instead. Chivalry and all."

"I don't know," Jason said. "I think I'd back Danny in a fight over Brian."

"Besides," I said. "You try stopping her once she's decided something."

"True." Gil pulled a chair of his own beside us and sat down, and Jason followed suit. "So what happens if they don't find anything?"

"Then I guess we try again," I said. "If you and Jason are up for another round."

Jason blew out a long breath, and Gil chuckled. "That may take a few minutes. But I suppose we could try, as a sacrifice for the team." He stared out at the mist. "It still doesn't feel right, just sitting here and waiting. Maybe we should all have gone."

I shook my head. For some reason I couldn't quite understand, that felt very wrong. "Someone has to stay with the shop."

There was silence for a few moments.

"So," Gil said. "Do you know why Danny broke up with you?"

"Why is that what everyone brings up when they want to make conversation?" I said. "Have you people never heard of tact?"

"I'm just curious!" Gil protested. "I mean, it's weird, right?"

"I thought so," I said.

"She's had plenty of time to discover your flaws. So why now?"

"If you must know," I said, "she says it's because I haven't thought about what I'm doing after graduation."

"Huh," Gil said.

"It's all right for her," I said. "She's got Apollo's. My situation is a little bit more complicated."

"I guess." Gil shrugged. "We've got another year before I have to think about that one."

"I've already got an internship lined up for this summer," Jason said. "At Google."

"I hear the food is great there," Gil said. "And you get free massages."

They kept talking, but I stopped paying attention. I watched the mist, strands of silver playing over one another, and thought about Danny.

Was that what she wanted? Someone like Jason? Obviously not exactly like Jason, but a hypothetical version of Jason who liked girls. Someone who had his shit together, in other words. Who had a job lined up, a future planned, a house picked out. That sure as hell wasn't me.

"Brian?" Anna said.

"Hmm?"

I looked up at her pretty round face, framed by blond curls. She smiled.

"I don't think I ever thanked you. For stopping the dragon."

"What? Oh." I shrugged. "I wasn't even really thinking properly. If I'd realized what I was doing, I would have run the other way."

"That would have been the sensible response," she agreed. "Instead of trying to take on a mythical beast with a bag of coffee."

"You don't seem... worried by all this." I waved a hand at the mist.

"I ought to be." Anna shook her head. "It all seems a bit like a dream."

"Hey," Gil said. "Here they come!"

Danny emerged from the mist, magic sword in hand, with Lisa following close behind her. They weren't running, but they were walking quickly.

"What—" I began.

"Nope," Danny said. "Nope, nope, nope. We're leaving. You two, back in the sex closet. I'll start the machine up again."

Lisa was pale, but her cheeks were flushed. Gil looked from her to Danny and back. "Come on," he said. "You have to at least tell us what's out there."

"Nope." Danny laid the magic sword on a table. "Come on."

Gil looked pleadingly at Lisa, who stepped closer and beckoned. He bent down, and she whispered in his ear at some length.

"—shaped like what?" he said, at one point, prompting more urgent whispers. Eventually he straightened up, a faraway look in his eyes.

"I would have liked to see that," he said.

"Gil!" Danny said, standing by the swinging door to the kitchen.

"All right, all right." Gil took one last look at the mist, then turned to Jason. "Well, dear, are you ready to do our duty by captain and crew?"

Jason heaved a mock sigh, and the two of them went behind the counter arm in arm. Danny stepped out of the way and ushered them through. A moment later, I heard the clack of the big switch on the magic coffee machine.

Lisa was whispering to Anna, who was blushing and hiding her face in her hands. I left them to it, and Evan to his sulking, and went back to talk to Danny.

She was standing behind the counter by the kitchen door, leaning against the back wall, trying to look relaxed while all four foot eleven and a half inches of her vibrated with tension. When I said hello, she jumped.

"What?" she said. "What do you want?"

"I just wanted to talk," I said. "Are you okay?"

"Fine," she said. "I'm fine."

"You don't look fine."

"Well, I am."

"Danny—" I reached out for her, but she batted my hand away.

"None of that. You could stand to take this a little more seriously, you know."

I blinked. This from the girl who, as far as I could tell, had never taken anything seriously in her entire life. "I am! I get it. This is dangerous."

"You don't get it." She ran her hand through her blue-and-purple hair. "Look. I don't mean to be shitty to you in particular, Brian, but obviously I'm a little worked up right now."

"It's all right," I said. "If you want to talk about it—"

"I don't want to talk about it. I just want to go home." She glared at the kitchen door. "Shouldn't it be working by now?"

"I wasn't timing it," I said, glancing at the front door. There was no static obscuring the mist.

"I'm going to check the machine." Danny pushed the swinging door open, and a moment later started swearing.

"What? What happened?"

"It's not fucking working!" she shouted. "It's just brewing a pot of god-damned coffee!"

We sat in a circle around one of the larger tables, with the pot of coffee between us. After a long silence, Gil got a styrofoam cup and poured himself some.

"You're not really going to drink that?" Evan said. "The magic sex coffee?"

"It's not sex coffee," Gil said. "And it smells good. I'm not going to let it go to waste."

He took a drink. We all waited. When he failed to magically transform into a badger or start glowing, everyone relaxed.

"It's just coffee," Gil said. "Not bad, though."

Jason helped himself to a cup. After a moment, so did Danny.

"All right," she said, sipping. "It didn't work. Why didn't it work?"

"I asked Twitter for opinions," Lisa said, scrolling her iPad. "So far I'm not getting anything really useful."

"Maybe Gil and Jason were too tired?" Evan said. "Maybe they didn't impress the magic coffeemaker this time."

"Wait, so now we're being judged on our performance?" Gil said. "All of a sudden I'm not comfortable with this. And for the record, Evan, tired or not, I—"

"Wait," Jason said, in his quiet voice. "Gil. How did you feel, the first time?"

"What?" Gil looked around the circle. "I mean, good?"

"I felt like there was something different," Jason said. "Like an... energy."

"Like static electricity," I said. "I got that too, when me and Danny were—"

"Yeah," Danny interrupted. "Okay. So where does that leave us?"

"I didn't feel that the second time," Jason said. "No magic tingle."

"I can believe that," Gil said.

"So, and I can't believe I'm saying this, maybe Evan is right. Maybe there's some... energy that gets used up."

"Each time has to be a new couple?" I said. "That doesn't leave us many options."

Everyone looked at Anna, who blushed furiously and said nothing. Danny coughed.

"Maybe it doesn't have to be two new people. It could just want to see a new combination."

"So it's a creepy voyeur magic coffeemaker?" Gil said.

"It's a theory," Danny said. "There's enough beans left to try it."

"So who's going to be the guinea pigs?" Evan said.

Another silence, as everyone tried not to meet anyone else's eye. Danny sighed and got to her feet. "Evan? Come on."

"Seriously?" he said, shooting to his feet. "Okay."

"I—" I began, then stopped when Danny gave me a look that would have melted glass.

"Gil, throw the switch once we're inside," Danny said.

"Got it," Gil said. "Come back out if you don't feel that special tingle. There might be time to put in a substitute player."

I watched Danny and Evan disappear through the swinging door, and tried to keep the anger off my face. Lisa went back to her iPad, and Anna turned her chair around to watch the front door.

"Sorry," Jason said. "I know that has to be hard for you."

"He doesn't have to be so enthusiastic about it," I muttered.

"He's always had a crush on Danny."

"Really? He never told me."

"Would you have told him?" Jason shrugged. "Besides, half the people who come into Apollo's have a crush on Danny. It comes with the territory."

This was a trend I had observed myself, but with my ex-girlfriend and my best friend in the sex closet it wasn't what I wanted to hear at the moment. I grunted.

Jason sighed and scratched his beard. "You know Danny's story, right? How she ended up here?"

"As much as she tells anybody," I said. "Her dad owned this

place, and she took over running it when he got sick. When he died a couple of years ago, she ended up owning it."

"Yeah. Think about that for a minute. She's your age, right?"

"Just about."

I twisted my lip. This lent further credence to the "Danny thinks Brian is an irresponsible fuck-up" theory. Here I was at twenty-three, tens of thousands of dollars in debt for a degree I wasn't sure would get me anywhere, and in the meantime she's been running a successful business while taking care of a crippled parent.

"I just don't know what I can do about it," I said.

Jason looked thoughtful. Before he could speak, though, Anna interrupted from the front of the shop.

"Hey! It's happening!"

We got to our feet. The green static was indeed fading in, replacing the mist. Jason, who'd been occupied the last time, watched in fascination as it peaked and faded away, leaving another scene entirely in its place.

"Well," Anna said after a moment, "at least it's a bit more colorful."

Lisa's iPad chirped as she took pictures.

This time, Apollo's had apparently landed in the middle of a swamp. Vegetation clung to small, muddy hummocks, with channels of stagnant water in between, covered in floating vines and algae. There were a few trees, but they looked limp and sickly, and other plants sprouted from them like blood-sucking ticks. These parasites bore huge, brilliant flowers, a riot of dark blues, muddy reds, and brilliant yellows. In spite of the bright colors, there was a vaguely unhealthy look to the whole affair, a sense of rot and decay that redoubled as the smell started leaking in. The ever-present aroma of coffee warred with the sick-sweet scent of overripe fruit.

"I'm not going outside for this one," Lisa said, lowering her iPad. "Someone else's turn."

"We might need to build a boat," Jason said.

Gil, coming out of the kitchen, took one look and made a gagging sound. "Florida again?"

"Florida's got nothing on this," I said.

"What I don't understand," Gil said, "is why we keep landing in such unpleasant places. How come we don't get cute little towns or something?"

"Maybe the magic coffee machine hates us and wants us to suffer," I said.

The door to the kitchen swung open, revealing Evan. He joined the rest of us, walking with a definite spring in his step that made me want to punch him very badly. I could hear water running in the bathroom.

"This one looks interesting," he said.

"It's a dump," I said.

"No, it's fascinating," Evan said. "Look at the flowers!"

"You're just saying that because you got us here."

"I have to agree with Brian on this one," Gil said. "I'm not really feeling the Swamp of Decay myself."

"Something's moving out there," Anna said.

We all moved up to the front door, looking out through the fronds and hanging flowers.

"Where?" Lisa said, iPad at the ready.

"Somewhere out there," Anna said, pointing.

"Like, a big something?" Gil said. "Are we talking crocodiles here?"

"I don't... think so." Anna squinted. "It looked like—"

A new sound reached us, a droning, buzzing sound, like a computer fan with a bad bearing. Now we could all see the movement, a wave of flickering, darting things hovering over the water, homing in on the shop. They were constantly in motion, so it was hard to get a good look at them, but I got the sense of flickering wings and spindly, dangling limbs. It was disturbingly familiar, and Gil got it first.

"Mosquitos!" he shouted. "Shut the door, shut the door, shut the door!"

They were mosquitos, all right, but bigger than any mosquito had a right to be, the size of terriers. I grabbed for the door, but they were on us before I could slam it, a storm of them pushing in through the doorway and flooding through the broken window. I threw all my weight against the door, feeling multiple impacts on the other side as the bugs hurled themselves against the glass. It swung home, bell tinkling, and one of the grotesque creatures crunched as it was caught half-in and half-out.

Unfortunately, the hole the dragon had made in the front windows was still available, and the huge insects poured through it, hovering and darting. The room turned into pandemonium, everyone ducking and swinging at the things with whatever heavy object came to hand. Lisa smashed one against a window with her iPad, leaving both glass and tablet stained with cream-colored ichor. Gil had a chair, which he swung wildly, and Jason had retreated to a corner, pulling his jacket over his head. Anna pulled off her coat and wadded it up, swinging it by the sleeves like a makeshift mace.

I grabbed a heavy cardboard sign advertising today's roast and swung it at any bug that came close, warding off a couple with glancing blows as I backed toward the counter. Evan stumbled in front of me, clawing at his back, where one of the things had settled. Its long proboscis was embedded in the back of his neck, and as I watched the body of the insect began to bloat and redden.

"Get it off!" Evan screamed. "Get it off!"

"Hold still!"

He ducked, just in front of me, and I took a good swing with the sign. The mosquito crunched, spraying bug guts and blood, and I hammered Evan to the ground for good measure. It's possible I swung a little harder than strictly necessary.

"The window!" Danny shouted. She was jumping over the counter, scattering the donation animals, grabbing the magic sword as she came. "Help me get a table up!"

Anna, closest to the window, ducked underneath one of the big circular tables and lifted it onto its side. Danny made her way across the room, sword flashing out with a crackle any time a mosquito got near her. Severed limbs and wings fell like rain. I fell in behind her, guarding her back with my now-dented sign and feeling exoskeletons crack under my shoes. When we reached the table, I dropped the sign and took hold of one end, and Anna gripped the other. Together, we lifted it up and propped it on the booth against the broken window. With nothing securing it in place, it was a pretty flimsy barricade, but it covered most of the hole. I put my weight against it, feeling it shudder with the battering of more bugs from outside.

"Right," Danny said, an odd light in her eyes. She raised the magic sword. "Now we just have to clear the place out."

Over the next few minutes, the seven of us—minus me, since I was holding the table in place—waged a genocidal war of extermination against the mosquito menace. Even Evan managed to get to his feet and take a few swings at the circling bugs. Fortunately, the electric lights fascinated the insects even more than the prospect of a warm meal, and Danny was able to stand on tables and cut most of them to pieces while they circled. With that accomplished, she ran back to the kitchen—crunch, crunch, crunch over the dead bugs—and came back with two rolls of duct tape, which she and Jason used to affix the table to the wall and make sure the window was completely blocked.

More mosquitos hurled themselves against the other windows, mindlessly battering the glass in an attempt to get to the light. I sat down in the booth, adrenalin draining out of me in a flood, and looked over the battleground. Here and there, an insectoid limb still twitched.

"'Scuse me a sec," Lisa said. "I've just got to go be sick."

This she proceeded to do in one corner. Danny sighed.

"I'd complain about the mess," she said, "but under the circumstances, I think I'll let it go."

I caught her eye, and we both smiled. Then, as though she'd suddenly realized what she was doing, she frowned and looked away.

"You're a dab hand with that magic sword, you know," said Gil, from the chair he was standing on.

"Thanks," Danny said.

"Have you got a broom?" Anna said, looking over the field of insectoid wreckage. "We ought to... tidy up. Or else I may end up joining Lisa."

There was a push-broom tucked away in the sex closet, along with a bucket and mop. Everyone helped push the tables to the edge of the room, and then we took turns shoving dead mosquitos into the corner by the door where Lisa had vomited, which Gil charmingly designated the compost pile. Danny filled the bucket with water—the tap still worked, just like the power and internet—and did a little mopping over the worst of the stains.

After taking my turn on burial detail, or at least compost detail, I sat down in a booth as far away from the still-drumming windows as possible. Evan, a napkin taped to the back of his neck in place of a bandage, sat down opposite me.

"I think this shirt has just about had it," he said, plucking at the gore-and-ichor-encrusted thing. "If I'd known this was going to happen, I would have packed some extra clothes."

"If I'd known this was going to happen, I would have stayed home," I said.

"Yeah." Evan watched Lisa, pushing the broom with one hand over her mouth, and shook his head. "I guess I would have too."

I still was not feeling exactly charitable, but some amount of sympathy twanged. "Are you all right?"

"I think so. Lost a little blood, but that seems to be it." He patted the back of his neck. "Hopefully the damn thing wasn't carrying demon malaria or something."

"Let's hope. I don't think Danny's first-aid kit includes holy water."

"Thanks, by the way."

I shrugged. "It seemed like the thing to do."

"I wanted to talk to you about Danny."

My residual sympathy evaporated. "Please don't."

"When we were in the closet—"

"Evan. Seriously."

"She gave me a blowjob, since you're asking."

"I am not asking."

"But she didn't seem excited about it. All business, you know?"

I put my head in my hands. "Why are you still talking?"

"I'm trying to be reassuring! I think she's still into you."

"You are the absolute worst reassure—reassurer in the history of the world."

"I'm pretty sure that's not a word," Evan said.

"Besides," I said, "all you're saying is that she's not into you. Which, I mean, obviously."

"Ouch. That hurts, man."

"Good."

Evan sighed. "I just wanted to say... I don't know."

"That you're sorry for going into the sex closet with my ex-girlfriend literally hours after we broke up in order to power some kind of magical coffee transportation machine?"

"Yeah. That."

"Okay. Apology accepted. Now can we please never talk about this again?"

"Fair enough."

"Guys?" Danny called, from the now-clear center of the room. "We need your input."

Once again, everyone gathered in a circle. Everyone looked at Danny, who gave a short sigh before stepping forward.

"Okay," she said. "Obviously, we can't stay here, unless anyone has an oil tanker full of bug spray they're not telling me about. That means firing up the machine again."

"Point of order?" Gil said. "How many cans of magic beans are left?"

"Three," Danny said. "If it comes to that, we can try it with regular beans, but we should assume those three are all we're going to get."

"We don't seem to have any way of controlling where we end

up," Jason said. "I looked the thing over, and there's no hidden panels or anything."

"No manual controls for the warp drive?" Gil said.

"Not unless you want me to try taking it apart."

"Let's leave that for a last resort," I said.

"Agreed," Danny said. "So we're going to have to roll the dice again. That means a new pair in the closet."

"There are $(n(n+1))/2$ pairs in a set of n elements," Jason said. "For seven of us, that's twenty-eight combinations, of which we've used up three."

"I'm ruling some of those out, though," Gil said. "Some of us are in a committed relationship here."

"And some of us are brother and sister," Evan said. "In fact, why don't you just leave Lisa out of this weird erotic math session entirely?"

"Evan!" Lisa said.

"What?" he said. "I don't want my little sister used for sex to power the warp drive, and that makes me the bad guy?"

"I would like to do it," Anna said. Everyone stopped talking to look at her, and she looked down and flushed. "With Brian. If that's all right."

I looked at Anna, who wouldn't meet my eye, and then at Danny, who locked her gaze onto mine.

"That works," she said. "If Brian's willing."

I swallowed. "Sure."

For the briefest moment, there was something awful in Danny's expression, as raw and painful as an exposed nerve. Her business-like mask slammed back into place an instant later, but that tiny glimpse tore something inside my chest. My heart flip-flopped like a dying goldfish.

"Great," Danny said. "Go ahead. I'll give you a minute or two before I throw the switch."

It was a good thing the sex closet was overwhelmingly saturated with the scent of coffee, I reflected, or it would be getting

decidedly stuffy from repeated use. I closed the door behind me
and Anna, leaving us in near-total darkness, close and warm.

"Are you sure about this?" I kept my voice to a whisper. "You
barely know me."

Her hands touched my shoulders, tentatively, as though she
expected me to bolt. "Yeah. It's just..." She took a deep breath. "I
don't have a lot of... experience. You know?"

"Oh."

"So just..."

I nodded, then realized she couldn't see me, and said, "Okay."
Groping in the dark, I found her arms and pulled her closer,
running one hand up to cup her cheek and guide me to her for a
kiss. After a moment, her mouth opened under mine, and she
pushed herself against me. Her breasts, larger and fuller than
Danny's under her white sweater, pressed tight against my chest.

I could see her in my mind's eye, blushing, half-eager, half-
scared. I put my hand on her side, and felt the rapid thumping of
her heart. She broke away, gasping for air, and leaned back against
the stacks of coffee, pulling me with her. I kissed her, from her
cheek down to the hollow of her neck and back again, and let my
hand stray down to the soft mound of her breast. She stiffened a
little, then relaxed.

I could see—

I could see Danny, looking at me, that one instant of honesty
on her face. I felt like someone had reached through my ribs,
grabbed a handful of viscera, and twisted. My erection, only
halfway there, wilted like I'd jumped into ice-cold water.

"Brian?" Anna whispered in my ear, when I paused. "Is
something wrong?"

"Nothing," I said, pushing her back against the coffee again and
trying to banish Danny from my mind. It was no good. Her face kept
sneaking in at odd moments, when I slid my hands under Anna's
shirt and over the sheer fabric of her bra, when she untucked my
shirt and ran her nails up my spine. None of it produced the desired
response; the patient was flatlined. Dead on arrival. I could feel the
magic, the strange, static tingling, but it didn't make me feel like it

had with Danny. It was a strange, crawling sensation, running over my skin, like many-legged insects.

"I'm sorry," I said, after what felt like an eternity. "I can't."

"What's wrong?" Anna was breathing hard. "Is it... is there something I should be doing? I don't—"

"It's nothing to do with you. I just... can't." I groped for the closet door. "We should see if there's still time to put someone else in here."

The outside light was bright enough to dazzle my eyes, so I couldn't see Danny's expression when she said, "Already?"

"I can't," I said. "It's not working."

"Not working like you can't feel the magic?" Danny said.

"Or not working like you can't get it up?" Evan chimed in from outside the kitchen.

"It's my fault," I said. "The magic is fine. I just..."

"Christ Almighty," Danny said. She was standing beside the magic coffee machine, staring at it worriedly. "We've still got ten minutes or so left on this. Who else is going to have a go? Evan?"

Evan, standing in the kitchen doorway, looked uncomfortable. "I'm not sure I can... I mean... we just—"

"Gil?" Danny said.

"I'm not going in there with anyone but Jason," Gil said firmly.

"Well—"

"Oh, for fuck's sake." Lisa pushed her way into the kitchen and shouldered me aside. "Out of the way."

Anna, who had appeared at the door of the sex closet after straightening up her shirt, said, "Wait. I'm not—"

"Neither am I," said Lisa, "but this hardly seems like a time to quibble." She stepped into the closet, and Anna gave a helpless shrug as she closed the door. Then, opening it again, Lisa added, "And no smirking, Evan. You and Brian are next up."

The door slammed closed, the kitten calendar flapping briefly.

Anna, unlike Danny, was not quiet. The rest of us retreated to the front room to get a little distance from the thumps and moans.

"Well, well," Gil said. "Little Lisa's grown up all right after all."

"Shut up," Evan said, hands over his ears.

"Do you know if she ever... you know. With girls?" I said.

"No. I don't know anything. I'm not hearing any of this." Evan stalked off to try and find something to stuff into his ears.

"I'm more worried about whether it'll work," Danny said, watching the swamp through the windows. "The coffee maker was halfway through its cycle."

I wanted to talk to Danny, badly, but she hardly spared me a look.

"What are you doing with Lisa's iPad, Gil?" Jason said.

"Just updating her Twitter for her," Gil said, tapping away. "So it reflects a full and complete record of what's been going on."

There was a particularly loud moan from the kitchen, and a thump as though something had fallen over.

"It's working," I said. "Look."

Green static fuzzed the swamp, getting stronger and stronger until the mosquitos and the rotten flowers disappeared in a mass of flickering pixels. Danny had the magic sword in her lap, clutching the hilt tight enough to turn her knuckles white.

The landscape that materialized as the static cleared was better than the swamp, but not by much. It put me in mind of some blasted Scottish moor, which I'd never seen except on the better class of BBC programs: an endless sea of grass and small rocky hillocks, with a tree here and there for variety. Clouds, gray with pre-dawn light, scudded past overhead, driven before a wind strong enough to rattle the glass in the windows.

"Great," Gil said. "Just great. Looks like a fun place."

"I don't know," Jason said. "It has a certain charm. Very romantic in the Byronic sense."

"I'm going to see what's out there," Danny said. She got to her feet and opened the front door, kicking the corpse of a mosquito out of the way. "If I'm not back in half an hour, avenge my death."

"What?" Gil said. But Danny was already letting the door slam behind her. He turned to me. "Was that supposed to be a joke?"

"A reference, I think," I said.

"The Simpsons," Jason said. "That was a good episode."

Lisa emerged from the kitchen, looking extremely satisfied with herself. "Did it work? Did we get somewhere good?"

I waved at the new landscape. "Somewhere, anyway."

"Wow. Watch out for glowing black dogs."

"Where's Anna?" I said. "I need to apologize a few dozen more times."

"Getting cleaned up, I think."

I went around the counter and back into the kitchen, where I could hear the sound of running water from the bathroom. I sat at the little table and waited. The magic coffeemaker glowered at me from the counter, the two remaining cans of magic beans sitting beside it. Two chances left to get home, or at least somewhere that wasn't a total dump. Given our progress thus far, I didn't like the odds.

Anna came out of the bathroom, looking like she'd just stuck her head under the tap. She tugged at her mass of blond curls for a moment, then gave up and sat down heavily in the chair across from me.

"It's going to be a mess no matter what I do," she said. "My hair, I mean. I need a brush and some conditioner. I think it still has mosquito gook in it."

"Yuck." I looked down at my sweat stained, ichor-splashed shirt, and winced. "Yeah. Look, I just wanted to apologize again. It really wasn't anything to do with you. You're beautiful, and you seem great—"

"I get it," Anna said, holding up a hand. "Danny, right? You guys just broke up."

I nodded. "You've probably overheard every other person here asking me about it."

"Yeah. I couldn't really help it."

"It's all right." I sighed. "Anything to add?"

To my surprise, she appeared to take this question seriously, cocking her head and putting on a thoughtful expression.

"You said she was mad because you don't know what you're doing after graduation," she said.

"Right. I guess I can't blame her. Who wants to go out with someone who might be living in his parents' basement in a few months?"

"Do you know what she's planning to do? After you graduate, I mean."

I blinked. "I don't... no, not really."

"She never talked about it?"

"No." I shook my head. "I figured she'd go on working here."

"I don't know her," Anna said, "and I don't know you. Maybe that makes this easier. But have you thought about whether she wants to spend the rest of her life working in a coffee shop?"

"I—"

It was one of those moments where you can feel the world shift around you, crystallize and reform along new, unexpected lines. I thought back to that conversation, the things she'd said. About my future. And the L word, the scary one, the one I hadn't been willing to commit to.

She hadn't been trying to figure out if I'd be making money, or if I had a job lined up. She'd wanted to know if what we had was worth enough to take a risk. And I'd told her, no, it wasn't.

"Oh," I said, out loud. "Fuck."

"You should talk to her," Anna said. "I think there's more between the two of you than maybe you realize."

I swallowed. "I think you're right."

It was half an hour before Danny returned, covered in bits of bramble and in extremely poor humor.

"I was trying to get down a slope, and I ended up in a pricker-bush," she said, in response to our stares. "There's nothing out there. Just hills and mountains and grass."

"It's better than the swamp," Gil said.

"We've still got two sets of beans left," Evan said.

"If we use up the last one, and end up somewhere really

horrible, we're going to regret it," Jason said. "I hate to say this, but this may be as good as we're going to get."

"What are you suggesting?" Danny said.

"We could load up all the food we can carry from here and start walking. See what we can find."

"Give up, you mean," Evan said flatly. "Give up on going home."

"Think about it this way," Jason said. "What if we try two more worlds, and end up with that swamp full of killer mosquitos again? Or more dragons?"

"I don't know about you," Evan said, "but I have a life I'm not ready to give up. I have family. I have plans. I'm not going to just abandon everything to... to tromp through some wilderness."

"You think I don't?" Jason said. He was quiet but intense, maybe as intense as I'd ever seen him. "I'm saying that maybe we're not meant to get home, and we ought to accept it."

There was an awkward silence.

"When you say 'meant'," Gil said, "are you referring to..."

"I have no idea," Jason said. "My personal metaphysical model of the world went out the window about the time we figured out that the magic coffee machine slash warp drive was powered by sexual intercourse. But I'm not going to rule out the notion that all this is by design. That we're here for some kind of purpose."

"If that's true," Evan said, "I'm going to find whoever planned this and kick his ass."

"I'm sure the gods are just quaking in their boots," said Lisa. "Assuming they exist, and wear boots."

"I was raised Unitarian," said Gil. "Do you think it's too late to convert to worshipping Thor?"

Having spent the past few minutes edging closer to Danny, I edged around the magic sword and whispered in her ear.

"Do you think we could talk? Alone?"

She turned to me and narrowed her eyes. "Do you really think you have anything to say?"

"Yes," I said. "I really do."

After a moment of silence, she nodded. While the others continued arguing, the two of us slipped toward the kitchen. I caught Anna's eye as we went, and she gave me a covert thumbs-up. Danny led me back through the kitchen to the storeroom, which had a door we could close behind us. It smelled of gasoline instead of coffee. Danny set the magic sword down, carefully, and turned to face me.

"Okay," she said. "Talk."

"I've been doing some thinking."

"Startling."

"And getting a lot of advice. Most of it bad."

"Also not a surprise."

"And I think I figured out a few things."

She looked quizzical. "Such as?"

"Such as why you asked me if I love you." Somehow, the word didn't carry the terror that it once had.

"Oh." She crossed her arms. "This should be good."

I took a deep breath. "What are your plans for after graduation? My graduation, I mean."

There was a long, strained pause.

"That," she said finally, "depends."

"You don't want to stay here at Apollo's, do you?"

"Would you?"

"No," I said. "I don't think so."

"My father worked behind that counter for almost twenty years," Danny said. "I've been doing it since I was fifteen. I could spend the rest of my life here, doing the same damn thing."

"But you don't want to."

"No." Now she took a deep breath, and I was astonished to see the sparkle of tears in her eyes. "Have you ever felt a future trying to attach itself to you? Like a big silent shark of thing, getting ready to swallow you whole. And if you let it, everything will be smooth, you'll just be guided along until you get shit out the other end as an old woman and wonder where the hell your life went." Danny shook her head violently. "Fuck that. I'm not doing it."

"I understand," I said. "At least, I think I understand. So far. Can I ask you something that I genuinely don't get, though?"

She nodded, expression once again guarded.

"Why me? I mean, you like me, or at least you used to, but what do you need me for? If you don't want to stay at Apollo's, why not just go?"

Danny set her jaw. "You haven't figured that out?"

"Obviously not. But we both know I'm not that bright."

She closed her eyes and rubbed them each in turn with her knuckle, then set her shoulders and looked at me square.

"Because I'm scared, all right? It's as simple as that."

"You?" I blinked. "You're not scared of anything. You weren't scared of the dragon."

"The dragon wasn't my problem." She waved her arm vaguely at the coffeeshop. "Sure, I could leave tomorrow. Maybe it turns out fine. Maybe I can't find work and end up homeless on a corner giving handjobs for crack. Maybe I get kidnapped and sold into slavery. But if it goes bad, I just know I'd be thinking, 'Great job, Danny. You had a perfectly adequate life, and you threw it away because you felt a little bored. You deserve this.'" She swallowed. "That scares me. The dragon wasn't my decision, I just had to deal with it. But fucking up my own life beyond repair...."

"So where do I come in?"

She closed her eyes. "I like you, Brian. I like you a lot. And we were lying there that night, and I thought... maybe this is it. This is my chance to get out of here without fucking everything up. Because if I like you this much, if I love you, and you love me, how bad could it be?"

"If I'd said, 'Oh, yeah, I've got something ready—'"

"It doesn't matter if you've got a job lined up or not. I just wanted to know what you were thinking, because—"

"—because if I wasn't thinking about it, it means that I'm a colossal fuck-up."

"No. It probably means you're normal. But it means I shouldn't hang my life up next to yours when you haven't got yours figured out yet." She opened her eyes, expression sharpening a little. "Also, I thought you might at least have considered whether you were moving away, and what effect that might have on our relationship."

"I get it."

She blew out a long breath and looked me over. "You know what?" she said, sounding a little surprised. "I really think you do."

"And for what it's worth, I'm sorry."

"It's not your fault. You gave me an honest answer. It just wasn't the one I wanted."

"One more question."

Danny sighed. "Go ahead."

"Why didn't you just tell me all this?"

"Try and imagine," she said, "if I'd told you that I was considering quitting my job and going with you to who-knows-where to figure out a new life. How would you have reacted?"

I sighed. "I would have freaked out, wouldn't I?"

"Probably. I figured breaking up with you would be easier for both of us in the long run."

"Fair enough."

Danny shook her head. "So we've got all that figured out, now that it no longer makes the tiniest bit of difference."

"Actually," I said, "I'm not sure that's true."

Danny paused, watching me closely. "What do you mean? Have you figured something out?"

"No. Well, nothing important. Not how to work the warp drive or anything. But Jason was talking about whether we were really meant to find our way home, and I was thinking about all of this, and... maybe this is what you wanted?"

"You think I caused all of this? Like I have subconscious magic powers and all this madness is a result of my lust for adventure?"

"No," I said, "I hadn't actually thought of that one. I doubt it's so straightforward."

"Pity," Danny said. "Because that would be awesome. I would be okay with the world arranging itself to suit me."

"I just meant... this is an opportunity, right? A chance for a life that's at least different from anything we could have gotten back home. Maybe that's what we're meant to find here."

"'We?'"

"Yeah." My heart trip-hammered, sending blood thundering past my ears. "That's the other thing I was thinking about."

Danny just raised one eyebrow, like a tiny, tomboyish Mr. Spock.

"I love you," I said, and managed not to stutter. "And whatever we end up doing, here or in any other universe, I would like to do it together. If you'll have me."

"You don't get to say that," Danny said. Her eyes were filling with tears again. "You don't get a do-over on this one."

I watched her in silence. She set her jaw.

"And what if I fuck it up? What if I fuck everything up? Are you going to end up regretting this?"

I shook my head.

"You..."

Danny lowered her head and took a step toward me, then another. A third step, and she was pressed against me, my arms wrapping automatically around her shoulders. She was shaking, sobbing, and I could feel her tears soaking my shirt. I squeezed tight, and didn't let go.

Eventually, when the tears had run dry, she tipped her head back, and I bent down to kiss her. It went on for some time.

"I'm sorry," she said, when she finally pulled away, "that I went into the sex closet with Evan."

"You had every right to. And someone had to volunteer."

"It was still a shitty thing to do."

I kissed her again, and she sighed and pressed herself against me. As she did, I felt something spreading over us, a strange, tingling energy a little bit like static electricity.

"Do you feel—" she managed.

"Uh-huh." I nuzzled her cheek. "I think the magic coffeemaker approves."

We somehow managed to get the door to the kitchen open without ever quite losing touch with one another, stumbling toward the sex closet with arms intertwined.

"Gil!" Danny shouted. "Put a can of beans in the machine and pull the switch."

"What?" Gil said. "Are you sure?"

"Trust me!"

I pulled the door to the sex closet closed, the kitten calendar flapping against it.

The magic was definitely back. It crawled over the hairs on my arm from where her hand rested, and crackled over my fingers when I put my hand on her hip. When we kissed, tiny sparks snapped and popped, and I felt my eyebrows frizzle. Her hands were busy, yanking my shirt loose and pushing it up to my shoulders. I broke away from her to pull it off, and she fumbled the buttons on her flannel free, leaving it hanging open and loose. We came back together like a pair of magnets, too hard and too fast, and our feet got tangled up.

I half-fell, half sat against the bags of coffee, and she settled into my lap, the top of her head resting against my chin. I pressed my face into her hair; she smelled of coffee, and sweat, and dead mosquitoes, but it didn't make any difference. She twisted her head, and I bent down to kiss her again, while my hands slid up the smooth skin of her stomach and over her slender breasts, rolling my thumbs across her nipples. We stayed like that for a long time, barely moving, her lips hot against mine, my hands sliding up and down as her hips moved, gently, rubbing herself up and down the length of me.

Her hands slid up the sides of my leg, then around to her waist, and I heard the pop as she undid the button on her jeans. Then her fingers slipped over mine, guiding my hand down, past her navel, pressing under the elastic of her panties. I curled my fingers in the soft thatch of her pubic hair, slipping bit by bit between her legs. When I touched her, warm and wet, she went as stiff as if she'd been struck by lightning. She moved her hips, and I pressed my hand against her. Danny broke off the kiss and leaned her head against my shoulder, eyes closed and lips slightly parted, grinding herself against my fingers as I worked them on her sex.

We stayed like that a long time, too, just the slightest swaying motion, our hips moving in time. She pressed herself harder against me, legs tangling and straining against mine, her back arching like a bow. Her breath came in gasps, faster and faster, until she turned her head and pressed her mouth against my neck, smothering an animal sound from deep in her throat. Her teeth just barely nipped my skin.

Then, still shuddering, she rolled off me and onto the coffee bags, her hands fumbling weakly at the front of my pants. I pulled them down, harder than I'd ever been, and she wrapped her legs around my waist, her hands interlocked behind my shoulders. When I entered her, Danny—Danny, who never made noise during sex, not even a moan—whimpered my name into my ear, and I replied in kind.

It was the best sex we'd ever had, bar none. Breaking all previous records. New high score. I felt as though I should be entering my initials somewhere.

"Holy shit," Danny said, all her limbs still wrapped tight around me.

"Yeah," was the best I could manage.

"Did I bite you?"

"Just a little."

"Danny?" It was Gil's voice, muffled by the door. "Danny, get out here."

"Shit," Danny said. "Now what?"

"We'd better go see."

There was a certain amount of confusion as we disengaged and sorted out our various bits and pieces in the dark. When we were decent, I opened the door, and found Gil in the kitchen, beckoning urgently.

"Come on!" Gil said. "There's a... a guy."

"A person?" Danny ducked back into the storeroom and picked up the magic sword, then marched out through the swinging doors with me at her heels.

The others were all spread out around the edges of the shop. In the center of the room was an old man in a long white robe, with pure, snowy hair and a beard you could lose a mouse in. He carried a gnarled staff, wore a sword at his belt, and was a dead ringer for Ian McKellan. When he saw Danny, he dropped creakily to one knee.

"Princess!" he said, in an Oxford accent. "So the prophecy is true. You've returned to us at last."

"Princess?" Danny said. "You mean me?"

He nodded gravely. "In the time of the eighth sun, the Lord Most Vile will be denied his final victory by a princess from another world and her companions. She will have hair the color of rainbows, and come bearing the Sword of Heroes. Her trials will be great, but her strength will be greater." He let his head droop until he was looking at the floor. "I never thought to witness your coming."

Danny looked at me, and smiled. I smiled back.

"Okay," she said, setting down the magic sword. "Hold that thought. Guys, can we have a huddle?"

Everyone packed back into the kitchen.

"What did you guys do?" Gil said.

"Oh," I said, elbowing Evan in the ribs. "This and that."

"This is where I'm supposed to be," Danny said. "You were right, Jason. This is my stop, and I'm getting off."

"I'm going with you," I said.

"The old guy said companions," Danny said. "So the door is open to anyone else who wants to come with."

Gil and Jason looked at one another. Then Gil said, slowly, "What's the alternative?"

"There's one can of beans left," I said. "I'm suddenly very certain that if you use it, it'll take you home."

Gil looked from me to the magic coffeemaker, and nodded slowly. "Okay. Speaking only for myself, while it might be fun to hang out with a princess, I'm going to get back to real life." He looked over at Jason again, and his voice cracked a little. "I understand if you want to stay, though."

"Don't be stupid," Jason said.

"Haven't you always wanted to live in Fantasyland?" Gil said.

"It's a nice place to visit," Jason said. "But I wouldn't want to stay. And I've got that internship at Google to think of."

"That's two staying," Danny said. "I don't want to hurry you, but let's not keep the old guy waiting."

"I'd like to come with you," said Anna. "If you'll have me."

"Of course," Danny said. "Are you sure that's what you want?"

She nodded. Something seemed to pass between the two of them that I wasn't privy to, and Danny grinned.

"Lisa and I will be going home," Evan said. "Obviously."

"Obviously yourself," Lisa said. "I'm going with Danny."

"You can't do that," Evan said. "It—"

"Enough," Danny said. "I'm the princess around here, and I say Lisa gets to decide for herself. Lisa, are you certain?"

Lisa took a deep breath and nodded. She handed her iPad to Evan, who accepted it numbly.

"Take this," she said. "I doubt I'll need it."

"That does leave the question of how we get back," Gil said. "Since Jason and I have already gone."

"Oh, that's easy," Danny said. "Just squeeze all three of you into the closet."

"Hrm," Jason said. "We never tried three-element solutions. That would open the space up quite a bit."

"Wait a minute," said Evan. "I'm not—"

"Is that really something to quibble over at this point?" I said.

Gil put his arm around Evan's shoulders. "Come on," he said. "What's the worst that could happen?"

"Right," Danny said. "Princess crew, fall in!"

She led the three of us back out into the front room, where

the old man had gotten to his feet. Danny picked up the magic sword and spun it through the air with a flourish and a crackle of power. Her blue and purple hair stuck up in unkempt spikes, her skin was grimed with sweat, her clothes sticky with mosquito ichor. Her green eyes were sparkling and brilliant. I thought she must be the most beautiful girl in all the worlds.

"Okay, Dumbledore," she said. "Let's get to work."

Contributors

Rebecca Croteau lives in the wilds of New England with her cats and her family. She writes erotica, romance, and dark fantasy, and was previously published with Circlet Press as R. Ann Sawyer. Her first dark fantasy novel will be available from Penner Publishing in May 2015. She tweets as @ReeCroteau.

Owen James Franks got started writing erotica the same way he got started with a lot of things: good friends, a happy hour, and a few espresso martinis. "...And Friday is Formal Day" is his first published story. He lives in the Pacific Northwest with his wife and five children, and generally does his writing in places that are quieter than his home office, such as coffee shops and jackhammer test facilities.

Justin Josh has worked as a carpet cleaner, fast-food worker, data entry clerk, bookkeeper, landscaper, singer, actor, radio host, television consultant, teacher and more. He writes in several genres including the paranormal, speculative fiction and gay romance/erotica. He currently resides in southern California.

An unapologetic farm girl and bibliophile, **Axa Lee** finds her bliss listening to audiobooks while fencing her grass-fed beef cows. While she might be weighed down by a herding dog who can't herd, she retains high hopes for the toddler learning to fetch. She's a staunch believer that everything is better with coffee, wine, or soaked in whiskey, especially if it's homegrown. When not making googly eyes at her beloved Spousal-Type Creature or in search of the next great book, she's usually cleaning various suspicious farm substances out of the carpet or someone's hair and daydreaming about people who only exist in her imagination. Her works have appeared in several anthologies and she's always looking forward to the next story.

K.L. Noone is a writer and adjunct professor of English, currently completing her PhD in the areas of fantasy fiction and popular-culture medievalism. She has published several fantasy and romance short stories, as well as more academic works on Welsh mythology, Arthurian legends, World of Warcraft, Joss Whedon, and Terry Pratchett. She also enjoys tea, comic books, and testing her husband's patience with obscure Star Trek references.

At 10, **JJ Poulos** was told that they'd never make it as a writer because their penmanship was so terrible. Since then, they've worked hard to become a troublemaker, an editor, a gardener, and, of course, a writer. Their speculative fiction has been published most recently in the Journal of Unlikely Cryptography and THEM-Lit. They reside in Madison, Wisconsin with their partner, child, basset hound, and chickens. Their handwriting is still terrible.

Greer Thompson lives in Seattle, Washington, where he deeply enjoys the cornucopia of trees and rain, as well as the sun for the 0.87 seconds it's out every year. He writes science fiction and fantasy at night and begrudgingly services computers for money during the day. "His Name Was Pumpkin Spice" is his first erotic publication.

Avery Vanderlyle credits her interest in the sexy side of sci fi and fantasy to reading Samuel Delany as a teenager. Today she still reads more than is healthy, devours Game of Thrones fan theories, plays Dungeons and Dragons, and earns money by making computer programmers cry. She lives in Boston with her spouse and six cats... some of whom converse with her regularly. Avery is excited to have her first story published by Circlet Press. Prior short stories appeared in anthologies by DreamSpinner press and Storm Moon Press. Keep up with her at averyvanderlyle.wordpress.com and on twitter @averyvanderlyle.

Django Wexler graduated from Carnegie Mellon University in Pittsburgh with degrees in creative writing and computer science, and worked for the university in artificial intelligence research. Eventually he migrated to Microsoft in Seattle, where he now lives with two cats and a teetering mountain of books. When not writing, he wrangles computers, paints tiny soldiers, and plays games of all sorts.

Titles you may enjoy from Circlet Press!

The Flesh Made Word: *Erotic Tales About Writing*
edited by Bernie Mojzes
ISBN: 978-1-61390-123-6
Price: $6.99

Ten writers explore the erotic possibilities of the written word, from a typewriter that awakens ghosts of desire, to a woman whose skin holds the stories of her lovers. An erotic fantasy anthology. Strip away everything external, and the act of writing becomes profoundly physical. What's more intimate than expressing the hidden self upon a surface, transforming it in the process?

Whispers In Darkness: *Lovecraftian Erotica*
Edited by J Blackmore
ISBN: 978-1-61390-034-5
Price: $6.99

Strange! Electrifying! Sexy! Eldritch? Explore the new and exciting world of Lovecraft-based erotica in Whispers in Darkness, a new collection from Circlet Press. This cyclopean collection features eight new stories each filled to the brim with insanity-inducing, orgasm-producing goodness. Just beware: what one has seen (and been aroused by) cannot be unseen...!

Titles you may enjoy from Circlet Press!

Things Invisible To See: *Lesbian and Gay Tales of Magical Realism*
Edited by Lawrence Schimel
ISBN: 978-1-61390-083-3
Price: $6.99

Top contemporary authors bring us these stories of the realms of spirit that underlie the mundane world. From comic situations to poignant tales of love and loss, these stories are about finding something more than life as we know it.

Masked Pleasures
Edited by Jennifer Levine
ISBN: 978-1-61390-006-2
Price: $6.99

This anthology of erotic fantasy features stories inspired by the cover photo. Writers were challenged to use the photo as their muse or inspiration and to let their imagination take over from there. The result is a collection of stories at once nostalgic and looking toward the future, finished off with a dash of hope and a sprinkle of romance.